GHOSTLY HOLIDAY

A Harper Harlow Mystery Book Eleven

LILY HARPER HART

HarperHart Publications

❀ Created with Vellum

One

"It's the most wonderful time of the year."

Zander Pritchett, his dark hair gleaming under the pink gel bulbs in the jewelry store, fixed Jared Monroe with a challenging look as they stood in front of the display case. There was a dare there, an "if you don't do what I say, I'm going to punish you" provocation.

For his part, Jared merely shook his head and studied the rings in front of him. When he asked Zander to accompany him so he could pick out the ideal token of affection for his girlfriend — he was determined to drum up the perfect Christmas proposal even if it killed him — he didn't see the harm in the invitation. Now he realized it was a mistake, but there was very little he could do about it.

"It's the most wonderful time of the year," Jared replied dully, his eyes flat as he studied an emerald cut solitaire that made him think of his girlfriend.

Harper Harlow was many things. She was gregarious, chatty, tons of fun, and strong. She didn't go for a lot of frills, so Jared was convinced that a simple ring was the way to go. Zander, Harper's best friend, kept pointing toward absolutely ridiculous offerings and declaring they were the way to go.

Basically, the two men were at loggerheads and it didn't look as if the tension was going to ease anytime soon.

"May I see this one?" He pointed toward the ring that caught his attention and the woman behind the counter — her name tag read "Laura" — smiled serenely as she jangled her keys and opened the door.

"Absolutely."

If Laura was bothered by the amount of time Jared and Zander had spent hopping from display case to display case, she didn't show it. In fact, the weird smile never left her features. She almost looked drugged. Of course, Jared rationalized, if he had to put up with hundreds of Christmas shoppers he would adopt a defensive expression, too. She was probably trying to find a way to survive the day.

"Here we go." Laura removed the ring from the case and handed it to Jared, allowing him to lift it and stare at the twinkling gemstone.

"This is kind of nice, huh?" Jared asked Zander hopefully.

Instead of agreeing, Zander merely shrugged. "I think it's boring. This one over here has a diamond and eight different other gemstones set up in a rainbow arc. That's much more exciting."

Jared heaved out a sigh and reminded himself that Zander was doing him a favor. While Jared and Harper had only been together several months — although they'd changed each other's lives in that time — Zander and Harper had been joined at the hip since they were children. They were the best of friends, so close they fought separation (even when irritated with one another). Jared wanted Zander involved in the process ... even if it meant Zander would drive him crazy until the proposal was on the books and Jared could refer to Harper as his fiancée rather than his girlfriend.

"She won't like that ring," Jared argued, his temper getting the best of him. "I mean ... it's ridiculous."

"It's unique," Zander countered. "Look at it. You've got a huge diamond, which is a necessity. Then you have an amethyst, ruby, sapphire, emerald, aquamarine, citrine, and tanzanite surrounding it. What's not to like about that? Harper is a unique person. She should have a unique ring."

"That ring is one of our most popular sellers," Laura offered, her smile suggesting she was trying to be helpful. "It's expensive, but worth it if you love someone."

Jared made an exaggerated face. "So ... basically you're saying that this ring isn't unique because you've sold a buttload just like it ... and that I'm going to make a rotten husband because I don't want to spend the money on that ring. Am I missing anything?"

Laura was blasé. "I was simply trying to help."

"Ignore him," Zander volunteered, making a clucking sound with his tongue as he shook his head and turned away from the garish ring. "He's nervous about becoming a husband. It's normal ... at least if I'm to believe what movies and television have shown me over the past twenty years."

Jared scowled. "Are you trying to drive me crazy?"

"I don't know. Is it working?"

"Yes."

"Then I'm trying to drive you crazy." Zander winked as he nudged Jared to the side with his hip and focused on the ring Jared had picked out. To both of their surprise, Zander didn't brush away the ring selection right away ... like he had with every other ring that earned Jared's attention.

"Well, this isn't terrible," Zander said finally, removing the ring from the velvet display and sliding it on his finger so he could look at it. His hands were much larger than Harper's, so the ring didn't make it past the first knuckle. Still, his eyes gleamed with interest as he studied the stone.

"What can you tell me about this ring, Laura?" he said after a beat.

"That ring was acquired through an auction," Laura replied, grabbing a clipboard from the back of the display. On it, the specifics of each ring were listed, and she appeared bored as she read them off. "It's a platinum setting, emerald cut, color G, and clarity is listed at VS1."

"How many carats?" Zander queried.

"Two."

Zander pursed his lips as he stared at the ring. "It's kind of nice," he hedged after a moment's contemplation. "The other one is more colorful. This one ... well, this one ... ." He trailed off, letting loose a sigh. "This one does kind of look like her."

Hope flared in Jared's chest. "You actually like the same ring as me? We've been at this for hours and that's yet to happen."

"I didn't say that," Zander shot back, haughty. "I simply said this wasn't terrible."

Shrewd, Jared narrowed his eyes. "I think you like it."

"And I think you're full of yourself." Even though he said the words with feeling, Zander kept the ring elevated and sighed. "She would love this ring."

"Seriously?"

"Yeah. This is her. I would love the other ring but this one ... it's simple but eye-catching. It's not so big it would overpower her hands, which are small. It's ... her."

Jared was so giddy he wanted to do a little dance. "I'll take this one." He snagged the ring from Zander's hand and shoved it toward Laura. "I want a pretty little box for it."

"Okay." Laura's expression was back to reflecting the monotony of the day. "Don't you want to know how much it costs?"

Jared hadn't even considered that. He was resigned to the fact that the ring would be expensive. He was prepared to pay whatever it took to get Harper the perfect ring. The moment of truth had him girding himself. "Lay it on me."

Laura told him in a flat tone that caused the color to drain out of his face.

"Wow," he muttered when he absorbed the total. "That's a lot of money."

"It is," Zander agreed, somber. "Harper would be okay if you got her a smaller ring." It was rare for Zander to be cognizant of other people's feelings, so his response caught Jared off guard.

"You're actually suggesting I buy her a smaller ring?" Jared was understandably dubious. "When did that happen?"

"I don't know." Zander held his hands out and shrugged. "I just keep picturing Harper's face when she finds out you signed yourself up for indentured servitude to pay for this thing."

Jared blinked several times and then shook his head. "It's okay. I've got the money."

"You do?"

He nodded. "I lived with my mother even after I got a job on the west side of the state. She thought it was stupid for me to buy my own place, so I helped with the bills and saved a lot of money. Then I moved over here, got a pay raise, and still managed to save for six months ... until Harper and I bought a house together.

"Originally, I had the money for the house," he continued. "I didn't think anything of buying it for both of us. Harper insisted that she contribute, so I spent less than I figured I would. I've got enough for the ring."

"So ... buy it," Zander prodded, brightening. "If you've got the money, you should totally do it. This ring is fabulous and Harper is going to love it."

"And you think she'll say yes, right?"

The question caught Zander off guard. "Are you honestly saying you think she won't? That's ludicrous. She loves you."

"I know. It's just ... with everything that happened." Jared trailed off. He didn't want to talk about Quinn Jackson, Harper's former boyfriend who came back from the dead weeks before. The memory of what happened, the fact that Quinn was never in any real danger and faked his death to get away with any number of illegal deeds, was still at the forefront of Jared's mind.

Harper had felt betrayed by Quinn's turn, angry that he bamboozled her. She'd been lovey-dovey since her former boyfriend's arrest, but she'd also been quiet. Jared worried that she was internalizing too many of her feelings and that would lead to an explosion, which was exactly what he didn't want on the eve of a proposal.

"Everything that happened merely put things into perspective for Harper," Zander argued. "She's fine. You'll see when you propose. She's going to fall all over herself because she's so happy."

"Are you sure?"

Zander bobbed his head. "I'm sure. You're what she wants ... even though I've tried to tell her you're a tool trying to steal her away from me. She loves you. She's going to say yes. And, as for the ring ... it's perfect."

Jared exhaled heavily, allowing some of the tension he'd been carrying for the past several weeks to ease. "I'll definitely take the ring," he told Laura. "Make sure the jewelry box is blue if you can. I want it to match her eyes."

"No problem." This time Laura's smile was legitimate. "I think your girlfriend is going to have a happy Christmas."

"I told you it was the most wonderful time of the year," Zander snapped. "Why does no one listen to me?"

ACROSS TOWN, HARPER GRUNTED as she lowered a huge crate of kitchen utensils and supplies to the counter of her new home. She had the day off — as head of Ghost Hunters, Inc., she'd discovered throughout the years that Christmas wasn't a busy time when it came to hunting ghosts — so she decided to transport several boxes between her old house (which she shared with Zander) to her new house. Luckily for her, the houses were directly across the road from one another so it wasn't a long trip.

"Does Zander know you took this stuff?" Shawn Donovan, Zander's boyfriend and the man who was moving into Harper's old house with her best friend, eyed the mixing bowls in the crate with a mixture of worry and suspicion.

Harper snorted at his expression. "Oh, you're looking out for Zander's mental well-being. That's kind of cute."

"He uses these bowls every day."

"Yes, but those bowls were a Christmas gift from my mother three years ago. She thought it was important I learn how to bake if I wanted to catch a man. They're mine."

"Oh." Shawn was mollified ... slightly. "You've told Zander you plan on taking them with you, though, right?"

Harper sighed as she smoothed her blond hair, which was slightly damp from the light dusting of snow that hit as they crossed the street. She couldn't blame Shawn for being worried. Zander had a tendency to freak out at the strangest of times. "Don't worry. I'll talk to him. It will be fine."

Shawn knew Zander well enough to have doubts about that statement. "He's already stressed about you moving. He might turn your taking the bowls into something to fight about."

"He's going to fight regardless. He won't be able to stop himself." Harper had already resigned herself to that. "I love him ... but he's a real pill. It doesn't matter how we bend over backwards to make him happy, he's going to melt down. Right now, I'd actually prefer to get it over with."

Shawn's expression turned keen. "You're trying to push him into a freakout on purpose. That's why you took a set of bowls you don't care about but he loves."

"I took the bowls because they're mine," Harper said evasively. When Shawn didn't immediately speak, she blew out a sigh and flicked her eyes to him. "And because I think we need to get the freakout behind us. Christmas is right around the corner. I don't want him being a pain on the holiday. That's like the last day we'll be living in the other house together."

Shawn wanted to laugh at her hangdog expression, but he managed to hold it back. "You know Zander very well. You always understand how to handle him. I think pushing him to melt down sooner rather than later is a good thing."

"You do?" Harper couldn't help being relieved. "He's been quiet, a little too helpful for his own good since the Quinn stuff. I want him to go back to being himself."

"What happened with Quinn shook him," Shawn admitted. "He never liked the man, but he didn't see the evil that was lurking right there."

"That shook both of us," Harper noted. "He can't internalize it any longer, though. It's time we got back to normal ... and he needs to melt down for that to happen."

"Well, in that case, taking the bowls was a masterful stroke."

Harper grinned. "I thought so. Just to be on the safe side, though, I'm going to take that crystal bowl on the living room table. My father got us that four years ago."

"That will definitely do it."

"I thought so. Let's make one more trip between the houses and then call it a day. We've almost transported everything between the houses. It's starting to get real ... and I want to save a little something for tomorrow."

"I can handle that."

SINCE JARED MEASURED HARPER'S finger when she was asleep — something that wasn't easy and he had to be sly about — he knew the exact size the ring should be. That meant he could wait inside the store with Zander because the jeweler did its own sizing.

Forty minutes after picking out the ring, it was sized down to fit Harper and the two men were ready to leave the store. Jared found his mood buoyed by the fact that Zander thought he was being an idiot for worrying about what Harper's response to his proposal would be. Since Zander knew her best, Jared was relieved that Zander found the question ridiculous.

"Okay. We've got the ring," Zander muttered to himself as they left the jewelry store. "What kind of wine are you planning on marking the occasion with?"

Jared had no idea how to answer the question. "Um ... the kind that comes in a bottle, right? I'm guessing wine in a box would be a big no-no."

The look on Zander's face was priceless. "Are you trying to kill me?"

"That's just an added bonus."

"You need champagne," Zander explained. "A really good champagne, in fact. I'm thinking Bollinger rosé champagne is the way to go."

Jared thought about arguing with Zander — he wasn't a huge fan of champagne, after all — but he ultimately nodded as he thought over the statement. Zander would know better what to serve at a proposal. "Can I get that locally?"

"I'll call around and order some if I have to." Zander was all business. "Where do you plan on proposing?"

"The new house."

"Why there?"

"Because that's where we're making our life together. I thought I would put together a picnic for just the two of us, tell her how much I love her in front of the fireplace, get down on one knee and ... do it."

"Do it?" Zander was instantly suspicious. "You're just going to do it? Please tell me you've been rehearsing the actual proposal and you're not going to 'do it' off the cuff." He used air quotes to let Jared know he was serious.

"I'm planning out the perfect words," Jared assured him. "I just ... haven't quite got them polished the way I want them yet."

"Uh-huh." Zander wasn't convinced. "Can I see the rough draft?"

"They're up here." Jared tapped his temple. "It's a mental draft."

"Oh, geez." Zander rolled his eyes. "Do you want me to write the proposal for you? I'll make sure it's romantic and exactly what Harper deserves."

Jared could picture the sort of proposal Zander would write and he wasn't about to agree to that offer. "I've got it. I know basically what I want to say. I just want it to sound pretty ... and perfect."

Zander's expression softened. "Because she's pretty and perfect, right?"

"Pretty much."

"Good man." He clapped him on the back and lifted his eyes to the sky as they exited the store. "It feels like snow. I don't think it will be a big dump — at least not yet — but it's definitely going to snow tonight."

Jared followed his gaze. "I like snow. Maybe I'll convince Harper to stay at the new house and we can camp out in front of the fireplace. That sounds like a great way to enjoy the first real snow of the year."

"No. Harper only has a few nights left in *our* house. I don't want you stealing one."

Jared bit back a sigh ... barely. "Fine. I won't steal her just yet. Does that make you happy?"

"If you wanted to make me happy we would all go in together and buy a castle," Zander replied without hesitation. "We would live together forever and have a Starbucks attached to a pub right inside the house."

Jared didn't miss a beat. "That's never going to happen."

"Which is why I'm settling for the new arrangement. I … ." He didn't get a chance to finish because an ear-splitting scream filled the air, causing both men to snap their heads to the east. "What is that?"

"Come on," Jared barked, sliding the ring into his inside pocket and breaking into a run. "Someone is in trouble. We need to help."

Two

Jared found the source of the screaming fairly quickly. It was a woman, and she was standing in front of the town's lone coffee shop, a bag clutched in her hand. The noises she was making were unintelligible, more guttural cries than anything else. She was so pale he worried she was about to pass out, so he acted instinctively and grabbed her arm.

"Ma'am, what seems to be the trouble?"

The woman's eyes widened to the size of saucers as she slowly shifted them to him. For a brief moment, Jared was convinced she wouldn't answer. Finally, though, she found her voice. Unfortunately, it was only so she could start screaming.

"Ma'am!"

"Her daughter is missing," another woman supplied as she moved from beneath the awning. "The little girl was inside with her, but she didn't like the crowd so she went to stand in front of the coffee shop. She's gone now, though."

Jared ran the words, which seemed simple enough, through his head, but remained confused. "I'm not sure I understand."

"This is Karen Brooks," Zander supplied, stepping forward. "She's a teacher at the elementary school."

Karen smiled at Zander and offered him a half-salute. "And Zander and I went to high school together."

"She once fought with Harper over being class president," Zander added. "Karen won, and Harper was sad ... although I have no idea why I felt the need to bring that up now."

"That makes two of us," Jared said blandly. "I need to know about the missing girl." His voice gentled as he turned back to the original woman, who had stopped screaming but was sobbing so hard her body shook. "Ma'am ... ."

"Ally Bishop," Karen supplied.

"What?" Jared was bewildered. "That's the name of the little girl?"

"No, that's her name." Karen pointed at the red-faced woman. "Her daughter's name is Zoe Mathers. She's three."

Jared's stomach twisted, although he couldn't exactly pinpoint why. "I'm sorry ... she's three? Why was she outside on her own?"

Ally's face was pinched as tears started flowing freely. "I ... could ... see ... her ... through ... the ... window." The words came out in gusty heaves. "She ... didn't ... like ... all ... the ... noise. I ... thought ... she ... was ... going ... to ... start ... screaming ... so ... I ... let ... her ... come ... outside. She ... was ... right ... here."

Jared blinked several times in rapid succession. The mother was almost a complete loss, which was to be expected, but he needed her to pull it together. Time was of the essence.

"What about people leaving the coffee shop?" Jared asked, his eyes on Karen rather than Ally. "Did anyone leave the coffee shop in the time Zoe was outside?"

Karen shrugged. "I don't know. I wasn't paying close attention. I do know Zoe was out here. You could see her. She was hopping on the cement and singing a little song. She had her pink coat on, and a matching hat with cat ears. She was adorable."

Jared exchanged a quick look with Zander, who seemed out of his element. "Okay, here's what's going to happen, Zander is going to call my partner Mel and get him out here. I'm going to start searching the street — including the back alley — and we're going to find her. She probably just wandered off."

"She ... wouldn't ... do ... that." Ally's lower lip trembled so forcefully it made her words hard to understand. "She ... just ... wouldn't."

"We still have to look." Jared was calm as he met Karen's gaze. "Take her inside and watch her, if you don't mind. I'm going to get as many people as I can to start searching. Odds are that Zoe simply saw something that interested her and wandered off. She's probably not far away."

Karen nodded, although she didn't appear pacified by Jared's words. "Okay. I'll do that." She grabbed Ally's arm and tugged her toward the door. "Keep us updated."

"We will." Jared was quiet until the two women disappeared inside the coffee shop and then he focused his full attention on Zander. "Call Mel right now and have him get as many people as he can to help with the search. Then start looking yourself ... and make sure you check everywhere. Little kids will climb under things, hide behind things. Leave no stone unturned."

"Okay." For once, Zander didn't balk at being bossed around. "What aren't you telling me, though?"

"What makes you think I'm not telling you something?"

"Because you've got that look. You know the one I'm talking about. It's the same look I get on my face when someone claims the *Will & Grace* reboot is as good as the first run."

"It's just ... I don't understand why anyone would let a three-year-old wander aimlessly by herself."

"She wasn't wandering aimlessly. She was standing right in front of the window. That coffee shop is small. It can feel claustrophobic this time of year because it's always packed with shoppers. I get why the kid wanted some air."

"Yeah, but ... ." Jared didn't give voice to his true fears. "We just need to find her. She can't have gone far. She's three, which means she has short legs. Get Mel out here and start looking. Hopefully we'll find her within twenty minutes. If she gets cold, she may wander out from where she's hiding on her own."

"Good point."

THREE HOURS LATER, THERE was still no sign of Zoe Mathers and panic was starting to spread throughout the community. Whisper Cove wasn't overly large. Given the number of people searching for the little girl, Zoe should've been found right away. The fact that she hadn't filled Jared with dread.

"Did anyone search the buses at the elementary school?" Mel Kelsey, Jared's partner and Zander's uncle, stood in the center of a group of volunteers and marked things off on a list. "Sometimes those doors can be forced open and a little kid would probably enjoy hanging out on a bus."

"I'll go," a man at the back of the assembled group offered, his hand shooting into the air. "That's a good idea."

"Make sure you get on each bus and look at each seat," Mel instructed. "If she was tired, she might've decided those benches would make for a good nap."

"I'll go with him," another man offered. "That's a big job."

Mel marked something on his map and focused on Jared as his partner closed the distance. "Anything in the alley behind the market?"

Jared shook his head. "No. We checked the dumpster, too, just to be certain."

"That was probably smart, although I don't want to think about that." Mel lowered his voice. "Ally is still inside the coffee shop. She's surrounded by a bunch of women trying to make her feel better. She's almost catatonic, though. I'm starting to think we should call a doctor or something."

The thought hadn't occurred to Jared, but now that Mel suggested it, he couldn't think of a reason not to do just that. "See if they can get someone out here to help us. I'm going to check that store right across the road from the coffee shop."

"The guitar store?" Mel furrowed his brow. "I think they would've said something if Zoe went in there."

"Probably," Jared agreed. "They have cameras, though."

Mel jerked his head in that direction, his eyes lasering in on the telltale dome over the door. "I didn't even see that. I guess it makes sense because guitars are expensive."

"I don't know that the camera would've picked anything up, but it's a possibility I don't want to ignore."

"No, that's a good idea." Mel brightened considerably. "You might even get a direction to focus on, although I'm starting to think the kid isn't down here."

"No." Jared rubbed his chin as his eyes searched the crowd. "Where is Zander?"

"He headed toward the lake with Jason Thurman." Mel was grim. Since Jason and Zander were always at each other's throats, things had to be serious for them to work together. "They're checking underneath Jason's balcony. There's a lot of stuff stored there for the winter. Also ... they're going to check the shoreline."

Jared read between the lines, understanding what Mel didn't want to say. If Zoe Mathers was attracted to the water, it was so cold and choppy that she wouldn't have lasted long. There was every possibility she could've washed up on the beach, which was a terrifying thought.

"What about the state police?" Jared asked after clearing his throat to dislodge the unhappy visual. "Can they get us a dog?"

"They're trying. They don't have any missing person dogs right now, if you can believe that. The only two dogs they have are drug dogs, which isn't what we need."

"No. Definitely not. I ... ." Jared trailed off when he caught sight of a familiar blond head. Harper, Shawn close on her heels, was pushing her way through the crowd. "Hey." He took a step away from Mel and pulled her in for a quick hug when she reached his side. "What are you doing out here?"

"Are you kidding?" Harper planted her hands on her hips. "This story is all over the news." She gestured toward the three local news vans parked along Main Street. "They've been doing live reports. A missing little girl right before Christmas is guaranteed to garner great ratings."

Jared rubbed his forehead. He'd seen the vans, but he'd been doing his best to ignore them. "Yeah, well ... I need to go across the street. Why don't you come with me and I'll catch you up?"

Harper agreed without hesitation, gesturing for Shawn to follow. "Come on."

"Where is Zander?" Shawn called out, drawing Jared's attention over his shoulder as they crossed toward the guitar shop. "Wasn't he with you?"

Harper knit her eyebrows. "Wait ... Zander was with you?"

Shawn realized his mistake too late to take it back. He was well aware that Zander and Jared went ring shopping together. He was purposely left behind to make sure Harper didn't wander into town and catch them looking at rings. He wanted to smack himself for letting the shopping excursion slip.

"I wanted to show Zander something I had my eye on for Christmas," Jared replied smoothly. "He knows you best, so I wanted to make sure it wasn't a stupid gift. And, before you ask, I'm not telling you what we looked at. It's a secret."

Harper snickered. "I can't believe you were shopping with Zander. That's so ... weird."

"Yes, well, it's our first Christmas together. I want to make sure you have the perfect gift."

Despite the serious nature of the situation, Harper went warm and gooey all over. "That's really sweet, but I don't need a gift. We just bought a house together. That's more than enough of a gift."

"Well, you're getting a gift, too." Jared was firm. "As for Zander, he's with Jason Thurman. They're searching the beach."

Harper didn't recognize Jared's heavy tone and made a face. "Why would Zander choose to hang out at the beach instead of helping look for Zoe?"

"He's not hanging out at the beach." Jared chose his words carefully. "He's looking to make sure that Zoe didn't end up in the water and wash back to the beach. They're also checking the area below Jason's deck. He's got a lot of outdoor stuff stored there that might interest a kid."

"Oh." Harper was mortified when she realized what Jared was really saying. "That's ... awful."

"It is," Shawn agreed. "I'm going to help. Hopefully they won't find anything out there, but you know how Zander gets when he thinks Jason is being annoying."

"Yes, he gets even crazier than normal," Jared said. "I think it's a good idea that you serve as moderator. I'll keep Harper with me."

"Good luck."

Jared opened the door of the guitar store and ushered Harper inside. She greeted the man behind the counter — who looked to be in his late twenties and was sporting some ridiculously long hair that would've made eighties rock bands stand up and applaud — with a tight smile. "Hey, Cooper. You haven't seen a little girl, have you?"

Cooper shook his head, his eyes reflecting worry as he tuned a guitar. "No. I heard about that and I went looking through the back alley. She's not there. I would've reported it if I saw her."

"I know you would have," Harper said hurriedly. "We're desperate to find her, though. We have to check everywhere."

"I'm actually here because I was hoping I could look at your camera footage," Jared announced, taking Cooper by surprise. "Does the angle you've got it set for hit the front of the coffee shop?"

Instead of acting as if Jared was putting him out, Cooper shoved the guitar to the side and hopped to his feet. "I didn't even think about it. I'm so sorry. Come on." He gestured for Harper and Jared to follow him into the office behind the counter. "I can't believe I didn't think about that myself."

"Don't worry about it," Jared offered. "Why would you think of it? It's just a notion I had. We might not find anything on the camera, but we should at least try."

"Definitely. Here." Cooper turned the monitor so Jared and Harper could see it. "I need to go to the playback option, which is here." He muttered to himself as he hit a few buttons. "Sorry. I only got this system because it was cheaper to pay for the equipment than my insurance premiums if I didn't have it."

"I didn't even think about that," Jared said, his eyes on the screen. "Wait ... slow down. There she is." He pointed at the tiny girl who hopped out of the coffee shop. She was far enough away that it was difficult to make out her features, but she didn't seem distressed. In fact, she was clearly laughing as she stomped in a mud puddle right in front of the door.

"What do you know about her mother?" Jared asked Harper, his eyes never leaving the video footage. "She seemed a righteous mess when I tried to question her earlier. I didn't have time to mess around, so I just left her in the coffee shop. I'm going to have to question her further if we don't find Zoe soon, though."

"Ally is ... I don't know what to tell you," Harper said, holding her hands palms out. "She's pretty together. She's not dramatic, keeps to herself. She seems devoted to Zoe. I've seen them around town. I wouldn't say I'm close to Ally, but I honestly think she's a good person."

"What about Zoe's father?" Jared asked as he leaned forward to the screen. Zoe was on camera waving through the window and then she went back to her hopping routine, clearly in her own little world.

"Zoe's father is another story," Harper noted, distaste evident. "He's a real ... ." She wasn't sure what word she could use without coming across as insulting.

"Piece of trash," Cooper volunteered when she didn't continue. "Luke Mathers is the biggest piece of trash out there. He's a terrible human being and Zoe's better off without him."

Jared widened his eyes. "Clearly I'm missing part of the story."

"You are," Harper confirmed, shifting from one foot to the other. "Um ... the thing is, Ally and Luke dated for several months about four and a half years ago. People thought they were a good match even though Luke has a certain reputation as a womanizer."

"He's hit more women than a female boxer," Cooper muttered, disgusted.

"He's a little gross," Harper acknowledged. "We always assumed that he would get over himself and settle down. A lot of guys are wild in their younger days and turn into perfectly good husbands."

"Okay." Jared felt as if he was walking through quicksand. "What aren't you saying?"

"Well, when Ally turned up pregnant, Luke had a bad reaction," Harper replied. "It wasn't completely unexpected. Even Ally said she knew he would melt down. She just thought he would step up to the plate after the fact."

"And he never did?"

"No." Harper's expression turned sad. "He's never met Zoe to my knowledge. He doesn't see her. He signed off on custody in exchange for Ally not going after child support. He completely abandoned Zoe. Ally has been raising her on her own."

"And doing a heckuva job of it," Cooper snapped, vehement. "She's better off without that loser."

"You seem to have some strong feelings on the subject," Jared noted.

"I was raised knowing that you take care of your children. You don't abandon them, no matter what. Luke abandoned Zoe without a backward glance. If you think I'm going to respect that, you're wrong."

"I don't respect it at all," Jared said, holding up a finger as he stared at the screen. "Go back just a few seconds if you can.

Cooper did as Jared asked, moving so he could see the screen as he started the playback a second time. "What do you see?"

"It's coming up." Jared was grim. "Right there." He pointed when Zoe jerked her head to the side. "Someone called to her, got her attention. And there she goes. Whoever it is, Zoe is going to him or her."

"How do you know it's a person?" Harper challenged. "Maybe she saw a dog or something."

"I guess that's possible, but I don't think so. Zoe was looking in the opposite direction. The way she turned makes me think someone addressed her directly."

Cooper played it again, and sure enough, upon second viewing, Harper was convinced Jared was right.

"So someone took her." Harper swallowed hard. "That means she's not out there waiting to be found."

"She's waiting to be found," Jared countered. "It just means someone is probably hiding her, which is going to make it that much more difficult to find her."

"Where do we look first?"

"I think the obvious place is with Luke Mathers. Perhaps he decided he wanted contact with his daughter after all."

"This is a sick way to get it," Cooper complained.

"There's no doubt about that. Come on. We need to talk to Mel and then I want to meet Luke Mathers for myself. I think we're going to have loads to talk about."

Three

Jared left Harper in town with Zander and Shawn — and Jason, even though the man still irritated him on a daily basis — and drove to Luke's house to question him. Once in a vehicle with Mel, he realized pretty much everyone in Whisper Cove felt the same way about the deadbeat dad in question.

"Slimy bucket of entrails," Mel muttered as he navigated the quaint streets. "I wish someone would castrate him."

Jared lifted his eyebrows, amused despite the serious situation. "Tell me how you really feel."

"I really feel as if he's pretty much the worst man in the world," Mel replied without hesitation. "I mean ... what kind of jerk doesn't take care of his own flesh and blood?"

Since Jared didn't know Luke, wouldn't be able to pick him out of a lineup, he decided on a pragmatic approach. "Are we sure Zoe is really his daughter? I mean ... I don't know Ally very well, but is there a chance he thought she wasn't his kid?"

"There was a DNA test."

"Oh." Jared was mostly mollified. "Why was there a DNA test if Ally never intended to go after him for child support?"

"Because he was telling anyone in town who would listen that she was sleeping with other people, something that mortified her. She was embarrassed — and I think there's probably a chance that she believed if she had proof he would change his ways — but he was even worse when it was proven that the kid was his."

"It gets worse?"

"He started making noise at the local bars, telling people that Ally probably drugged him so she could eradicate his defenses and purposely got pregnant with Zoe to trap him."

"That's kind of low, although ... is it possible she drugged him?"

"You don't understand. Ally is a good girl. She volunteers her time at all the festivals and even delivers food for seniors with Meals on Wheels. She's not a bad girl."

"Even good girls make mistakes."

"Drugging someone is not a mistake."

"Fair enough." Jared's mind was busy. "I don't understand why she let Luke off the hook for child support if she was certain he was the father. In her position, I would've dragged him to court and gotten every dime I could."

"That's not how Ally is. She's ... sweet, and doesn't like to fight. She keeps to herself and never causes problems. She never confided in me or anything, but I have a feeling it wasn't worth the effort for her. She didn't want to hold on to a man who didn't want her back.

"He did it to her, broke her heart, and left her with a parting gift of sorts," he continued, his lips twisting into a grimace. "She's not the type to want retribution. If she went after child support, then Luke would've been granted visitation. Given the way he treated Ally, she was probably afraid that he would be mean to Zoe."

Jared couldn't imagine anyone being mean to a small child, but he knew it happened. He knew worse happened. "If he didn't want anything to do with the kid, why would he take her?"

"I can't answer that for you. We don't know that he did take her. It could've been someone else."

"But ... why?"

"We both know the terrible reasons someone might take a child." Mel was grim. "Let's hope we're dealing with someone who simply wanted a child and not the other possibilities. It is close to Christmas. Maybe someone was feeling lonely and saw an opportunity."

"That would be the best-case scenario," Jared agreed. "The odds of Zoe being hurt by an individual who is lonely and looking for company are low compared to ... well ... you know."

"Yes. That's why we're hoping that Luke decided to become a father, and did it in a terrible way, or there's some lonely woman out there who wants to dote on a kid. If it's something else ... I don't even want to think about that just yet."

"Let's focus on Luke," Jared suggested. "He's our best bet."

IT WAS A GOOD THING Mel and Jared weren't expecting a warm welcome, because when Luke opened the door, he practically slammed it shut in their faces.

"Oh, geez. What do you guys want?"

Mel was calm as he regarded the blond man standing in front of him. "Can we come in?"

"That depends on what you're here for," Luke replied. "I don't want to donate to any police gala fund or anything, so if you're selling tickets, you can move right along."

Mel didn't as much as crack a smile. "We're here about Zoe."

For a moment, Luke's veneer cracked. It was brief, but Jared recognized a sliver of something he couldn't quite identify before the man turned jovial. "What? Does she need Christmas presents or something? Is this one of those 'Shop With a Cop' things?"

"No. If she needed gifts, I would simply buy her gifts." Mel's ire was on full display. "I wouldn't bother you over something a real man was needed for. You can be sure of that."

Luke's green eyes flashed dark. "Why are you here?"

"Zoe is missing," Jared interjected, legitimately worried Mel would lose his cool and pop Luke in the face rather than ask the questions they needed answers for. "We need information from you."

"What do you mean she's missing?"

"I mean that someone took her and now we need to find out who that someone is."

False bravado fleeing, Luke pushed open the door and allowed Mel and Jared entrance. Jared gave the house a long scan, his eyes taking in the empty beer bottles on the kitchen counter and the empty pizza boxes stacked on the floor in the corner.

"I don't understand," Luke said as he led them into the kitchen, grabbing the two nearest beer bottles and shoving them in a cardboard container. "How did she go missing?"

"She was downtown with Ally," Mel replied. "She was standing in front of the coffee shop, hopping up and down, when something drew her attention. We have her on camera, and someone very clearly said something to get her to look in that direction. Then she took off, and we haven't found her."

"But ... who would take her?"

"Why do you think we're here talking to you?" Mel challenged. "On our list of people who might want to do Zoe harm, you're pretty much at the top."

Luke reared back as if he'd been struck in the face. "I don't want to hurt her."

"You clearly don't want to take care of her either," Mel shot back. "When was the last time you saw her?"

"I don't see her." Luke swallowed hard. "I've never technically been introduced to her. I guess I've seen her and Ally in town a few times, like at that big pumpkin carving thing they had around Halloween. I saw her that day. Ally was helping her carve a pumpkin."

"Did you talk to her?" Jared asked.

Luke shook his head. "No. She doesn't know who I am. Ally said she wouldn't tell her until she was old enough to start asking questions. I stay out of their way because ... well, because it's what seems best for both of them."

"Yes, you're a real prince," Mel drawled. "Has anything changed about your relationship with Ally in recent months? I mean ... has she decided to take you to court for back child support or something?"

"Why not ask her that?"

"Because she's ... very upset," Jared replied, remembering the woman who could barely form words in the face of her daughter's disappearance. "She's having trouble holding it together."

"Well, then maybe she should've paid more attention to the kid." Luke's tone was biting. "If she'd been watching Zoe, she wouldn't have lost her in the first place."

Jared instinctively grabbed Mel's arms before his partner could pummel Luke's face. "Don't," he hissed, his eyes flashing with warning. "It's not worth it. I need you to help me find Zoe. If you go to jail for assault, I'm going to be on my own. Neither of us wants that."

Mel looked as if he was going to argue the point, but instead he made a disgusted sound in the back of his throat and turned away. That left Jared to finish questioning Luke.

"What's your status right now?" he asked after a beat. "I mean ... have you been dating anyone? Have you been shooting your mouth off in the bar to anyone? Have you been considering going back to Ally?"

The last question clearly flabbergasted Luke. "Why would you ask that?"

"Because I need to know." Jared refused to back down. "If you were sniffing around again and Ally cut you off, it might be motivation enough for you to take Zoe to make her suffer."

"I didn't take Zoe. I wouldn't do that to Ally."

"Oh, that's so sweet," Mel deadpanned. "You've finally drawn a line in the sand that you won't cross when it comes to hurting that poor woman."

"Hey! If you think I feel good about everything that happened, you're wrong," Luke spat, his cheeks flushing with color. "That isn't what I wanted. She knew I didn't want a family, though. I'm not the settling down type. That's on her."

"Yes, she got pregnant all on her own."

"Oh, you don't understand." Luke made a dismissive gesture as he turned his back to them, his shoulders heaving. "Ally and I have an agreement. I don't have to pay child support and she doesn't have to share Zoe. I don't interact with either of them. I'm holding up my end of the bargain."

"And what about any relationships you've been involved in?" Jared asked, calm. "Have you been dating a woman who might see Zoe as a threat?"

"I never date anyone seriously," Luke replied. "I sometimes date the same person for a few weeks, although I never go over three months, and that hasn't changed since before Ally."

"You dated Ally for longer than three months." Mel's voice was quiet. "That's why everyone thought you were finally gearing up to settle down. I bet Ally thought that, too."

"Well, Ally was wrong."

"She certainly was."

Luke heaved out a long-suffering sigh. "I know what everyone in this town thinks of me. I'm not an idiot. As for dating, I go out with women from time to time, but it never gets serious."

"Who was your most recent un-serious date?" Jared asked.

"Jessica Hayden."

Jared furrowed his brow. "Why does that name sound familiar?"

"She's a crisis counselor," Mel supplied. "You met her a few weeks ago when Annabelle Lipscomb died in that car accident on County Line Road. The kids at the school were in crisis and she spent an entire day up there with them."

"Oh, right." Jared bobbed his head. "Now I remember. She seemed like a nice woman."

"Which begs the question of why she was dating Luke," Mel spat. "I'm guessing it's because — like every other woman who has been stupid enough to take him on — she probably figured she was going to be the one to make him change."

"You're not far off," Luke agreed. "She kept wanting me to talk about my feelings and make plans for the future. We didn't have a future. She just couldn't see it."

"How did she take the breakup?" Jared asked. "Was she bitter?"

"She was surprised. I could see that. She wasn't bitter, though. She just told me I was a jerk and left. That's pretty tame for some of my breakups."

"Yeah, well, we're going to need a list of all the women you've dated for the past two years," Mel said. "We're probably not looking at them as the guilty party, but we need to be certain."

"Fine. Anything else?"

"That will be it for now," Mel replied. "Well, other than searching your house, I mean."

"Why are you searching my house? Do you really think I have Zoe here, stashed in some room, perhaps gagged and tied up or something?"

"We're going to make sure you don't," Mel said. "Do you have a problem with that?"

Even though he was clearly frustrated, Luke read the determination on Mel's face and merely threw his hands in the air. "I don't think I have a choice. Knock yourself out."

HARPER WAS FROZEN SOLID when she returned to the coffee shop after searching the beach with Jason, Zander, and Shawn. The endeavor took longer than she imagined — the beach seemed much smaller when it was sunny and warm — and she didn't bother grabbing gloves before leaving the house.

"Oh, that smells heavenly," she intoned as the woman behind the counter handed her a gingerbread latte. "I want to kiss you this smells so good."

Rose McGovern, the owner of the shop, merely smiled. "You were out looking for the little girl. I think you deserve a reward for that."

"I didn't find her." Harper rolled her neck and looked to the corner table where Ally sat with two women, staring into nothing as they tried to cajole her into talking. "How is Ally?"

"Not good," Rose replied, keeping her voice low. "She's no longer speaking, for the most part. She hasn't said a word in at least an hour."

"And before?"

"She babbled a bit. She said that Zoe liked going to the park and she was determined to go there and find her. Karen stopped her from leaving, though, and went herself. The park, for the record, has been searched three separate times."

"Well, that's not necessarily a bad idea," Harper noted. "If Zoe is out there wandering around on her own, she might be hitting different spots at different times."

The look Rose shot Harper was full of pity. "Oh, honey, you know she's not out there on her own. There's no way. The entire town is looking for her."

"I know." Harper felt sick to her stomach as she sipped the latte. "Someone took her, Rose. I saw the video. The angle is bad, so you can't see exactly who called to her, but it was obviously someone she knew."

"I wish I'd paid better attention. It was busy, though. The town is always busy with shoppers this time of year. I saw her a few times through the window. She looked to be having a good time bouncing around. You know how kids are. They find enjoyment in the oddest things."

"It's not your fault. It's not anybody's fault but the person who took her."

"What kind of sick loser would take a child before Christmas?" Rose hissed.

"I don't think it would be less worrisome if she disappeared in the middle of summer."

"No. You know what I mean, though. It's just ... this is supposed to be the happiest time of the year. Kids like Zoe are supposed to be dreaming about visits from Santa Claus and baking cookies for his visit. They're not supposed to be worried about being taken from the street."

Harper was thoughtful as she thought back to the video footage. "I couldn't see Zoe's face very clearly, but she almost looked as if she recognized whoever called out to her. I don't suppose you know who Ally spends her time with, do you?"

"Ally stops in here at least twice a week. She always has Zoe with her, and the little girl gets a cake pop and a hot chocolate. Then they sit in the window seat and talk about stuff, like unicorns and the elves working in Santa's workshop. That's what they were talking about the other day.

"Usually, Zoe is perfectly fine in here and never puts up a fuss," she continued. "Today, though, she didn't like all the people. Marge Hefferman was in here and talking at the top of her lungs. You know what that's like."

Harper nodded knowingly. "I do. She makes Zander look demure."

Rose snorted. "Yes, well, he was a hero today, too. He was out there for hours looking. He's not a bad boy, even if he is dramatic and loud."

"I would fight to the death with anyone who thought otherwise," Harper agreed. "Basically you're saying that you don't know who Ally spends her time with, right?"

"I'm saying that Ally spends all of her time with Zoe," Rose replied. "I mean ... I'm sure she has friends. She's not the wallflower type. Zoe is the beginning and end of her world, though. She's a wonderful mother.

"Sometimes ... sometimes I think that Ally dotes on Zoe so much because she feels as if she did wrong by the little girl when it came to picking her father," she continued. "Luke is the worst man alive, so Ally has to be the best mother ever to grace the Earth. I don't know how to explain it."

Surprisingly, Harper found she had a lump in her throat. "We're going to find Zoe. Don't give up. Jared and Mel are on the case. They know what they're doing."

"They do, but we all know the statistics. The things that could be happening to that little girl ... ." Rose's eyes filled with tears.

"Don't think that way." Harper's voice was low, guttural. "You don't know that's what happened. It's Christmas. People get lonely around Christmas. Maybe someone lost a child ... or had a mental break of some sort. It's possible that Zoe is fine, merely lost for a little bit."

"Yeah, well, I never thought I would be hoping for a crazy person to have her," Rose said, sighing as she grabbed the pot of coffee from the warmer. "I need to take this around. Help yourself to whatever you want. I think we're all going to need to keep caffeinated for this one if we expect to find Zoe."

Harper had the same feeling.

Four

Harper stayed at the coffee shop for hours, to the point where she was one of the few left. Even Zander and Shawn departed hours before she did.

Harper couldn't stand the idea of abandoning Ally, but she was at a loss of what to do.

"I don't want to be the rude jerk that kicks her out, but I can't stay open," Rose noted as she leaned against the counter. "What do you think we should do?"

"I don't know." Harper stared at Ally for a long time. She was alone at the table, staring into nothing, and the vacant energy hovering around the woman was almost painful to bear witness to. "Maybe I should see if she wants to come to the house with me. That way she wouldn't be alone."

Rose cast Harper a sidelong look. "I don't want to tell you your business, but I don't think sharing a roof with Zander is going to settle her."

"Yeah." Harper rubbed her cheek and opened her mouth to suggest Rose take her when the door to the coffee shop opened. Whatever she was about to say fled because she recognized the figure standing in the doorway.

Shana Hamilton, one of the most famous faces in Whisper Cove, briefly locked gazes with Harper before focusing on Ally. She didn't force a smile, which was probably wise, and instead moved to the table and sat directly next to the traumatized woman.

"Well, this is interesting," Rose muttered.

Harper couldn't help but agree. "Yeah. I ... ." The door opened again, interrupting her, although this time the figure standing there wasn't a surprise.

"Hey, Heart," Jared said as he stepped into the coffee shop. He looked exhausted, beaten down, and ready for bed. "I went to the house, but you weren't there. I think it's time you called it a night."

Agitation she didn't know was previously there bubbled up. "We can't just quit."

"We're not *quitting*," Jared countered. "We're ... taking stock for the night and starting again tomorrow. There's nothing more we can do right now."

"But ... ." Harper wasn't keen on the search being abandoned — even for a few hours — but she couldn't very well give voice to her fears in front of Ally.

Jared flicked his eyes to the table and the sympathy on his face was profound. "I didn't realize she was still here. She can't stay here." He moved to take a step in Ally's direction, but Harper grabbed his arm to stop him.

"Just ... don't." She exchanged a quick look with Rose, who was clearly thinking the same thing she was. "Shana might be able to help Ally in ways that we don't understand."

"Oh, yeah?" Since he was fairly new to Whisper Cove, Jared obviously wasn't aware of the story. It happened long before his arrival in town. "How?"

"I'll tell you on the way home." Harper licked her lips. "Maybe Shana can lock up for you on her way out, Rose. You shouldn't have to stay and I know you're worried about kicking her out, but this might be a nice compromise."

"I guess, although that will just mean I have to listen to Shana tell wonderful tales about her locking-up acumen for months after." Rose didn't look happy with the suggestion, but her resignation was obvious. "You get going. You've done enough for one day. I'll handle this."

"Are you sure?"

"I'm sure." She turned her eyes to Jared. "Get a good night's sleep so you can find that girl in the morning. That's the most important thing."

Jared nodded. "That's the plan."

JARED WAITED UNTIL THEY WERE in his truck and heading home to ask the obvious question.

"Who is the woman in the coffee shop?"

"Shana Hamilton."

"Why do you think she's powerful enough to help Ally through the most traumatic event of her life?"

"Because she's been through it herself."

Jared was taken aback. "What do you mean?"

"It happened years ago," Harper explained, searching for the right words as she held her hands in front of the heating vents. She'd picked up a chill while searching for Zoe and she'd yet to overcome it. "She had a daughter. Her name was Chloe. She was sixteen when she disappeared. That's when Zander and I were in middle school. Chloe was three years ahead of us, if I remember correctly."

"What happened?"

"It's a mystery. Chloe was popular, pretty, and recently elected homecoming queen. She was blond and looked like a model. Zander used to joke that he would go straight for her."

Jared made a face. "That sounds lovely."

"It was just a joke. Back then, Zander was still ... struggling ... with who he was. He's always been strong, but life in a small town would've been easier for him if he wasn't gay. Most people didn't have a problem with it, but there are always some people who just can't live and let live, if you know what I mean."

"I understand, and I wouldn't wish feelings of inadequacy on anyone. That includes Zander, who often goes out of his way to make my life hell."

"He enjoys messing with you. He'd stop if you wouldn't make it so easy."

"Yeah, well, let's focus on this Chloe girl. What happened to her? Could it tie into what happened today?"

Harper tilted her head to the side, considering. "I don't see how," she said finally. "Chloe was older. Most people assume she was taken because of her beauty, although the police had precious few clues at the time. I remember because Mel was on the case and he was frustrated. No one saw Chloe after she left school one day. It was in the spring; I remember that because the search weather was hit-or-miss. She was on her way home and never made it."

"No body was ever found?"

"No."

"Perhaps she ran away."

"Maybe, but I don't think so. Chloe was close with her mother. She wouldn't have run away like that. Besides, this was almost fifteen years ago. I think she would've gotten over whatever teenage angst was fueling her back in the day and showed up by now, don't you?"

"In theory, yes," Jared confirmed, pulling into the driveway. "We don't know what was going on inside that house, though. Maybe Chloe wanted to get away from her mother."

"Why?"

He shrugged. "Maybe Shana was abusive or something."

"I think people would've noticed that. Besides, Shana was a doting mother. She went to all of Chloe's cheerleading competitions ... and chaperoned dances ... and attended parent-teacher conferences. If she was abusive, she hid it well."

"Maybe something else was going on. What about Chloe's father?"

"I ... don't know." Harper searched her memory. "I can't remember what the deal was with him. I want to say he died when Chloe was little, but I'm not sure that's true. It's possible he simply abandoned the family. You'll have to ask Mel about that one."

Jared had every intention of questioning Mel further. "So, you think Shana will be able to help Ally, huh? Perhaps talk her down from the edge."

"I don't know that anything short of Zoe's miraculous return is going to help Ally. Shana donates her time to missing children organizations now. She's a familiar face on television when these cases inevitably pop up in the area."

"It's nice that she managed to turn her tragedy into something good," Jared noted. "Still, we need Ally to get it together. She's the one who can best answer our questions, and she's an absolute wreck. It's not as if Luke knows who was sniffing around Zoe."

Harper hopped out of the truck and waited for Jared in front of it. He'd clearly had a rough day and needed comfort. "I'm sorry you had to talk to him." She opened her arms so she could hug him, sighing when he wrapped his arms around her waist and buried his face in the hollow of her neck. "Tell me about your day," she whispered.

"There isn't much to tell. We've searched everywhere. This town is tiny. There's nowhere that kid could be hiding. Everyone rallied to find her and we came up empty."

"You think someone took her."

"I do."

"Then we haven't searched everywhere." Harper was calm even though her heart ached at the thought of Zoe spending the night locked in a dark room, which is exactly how things played out in her head. "We'll go door-to-door tomorrow and ask for voluntary searches. We'll get organized."

"I'm not sure that's a good idea." Jared swayed back and forth, as if dancing to a song only he could hear. "If our kidnapper gets word that's happening, what's to stop him or her from panicking and killing Zoe to keep her quiet?"

"We might get lucky."

"And we might not."

Harper hated how defeated he sounded. "Well ... what other options do we have?"

"I don't know. I need to think on it."

"Then I'll help you think." She pressed her lips to his cheek. "We'll find her. I have faith."

"I hope you're right. It's not going to be a merry Christmas for anybody if we don't find that kid."

"We'll find her."

They stood together, quiet, and absorbed each other's warmth and strength. The moment was exactly what they needed.

And then Zander opened the door and called out to them.

"Don't do it in the yard. Are you animals? We've been waiting for you and have dinner prepared. It's going to get cold if you don't get your bottoms in here."

Jared sighed as he rubbed his cheek against her head. "Just think. In a few days, we're going to be living across the road and we'll have no one to greet us this way after work."

Harper snorted. "You don't think his voice can carry across the road?"

"Good point."

"ANYTHING?"

Shawn didn't wait for Harper and Jared to get comfortable at the dinner table before asking the question.

"Not yet," Jared replied, rubbing his hand over Harper's back as Zander carried a huge tray to the table. "What's that?"

"Roast chicken, potatoes, and carrots," Zander replied. "It's comfort food. I thought we could all use it."

"Actually, you have no idea how excited I suddenly am for dinner." Jared's stomach picked that moment to growl, causing everyone to laugh. The nervous chuckle was enough to kill some of the tension hanging over the table.

"You can have first dibs on what you want," Zander offered. "I have a feeling you've had a long day."

"We've all had long days," Jared argued, although he accepted the huge spoon Zander handed him. "You guys spent hours searching the town. I had to run back to the coffee shop to drag Harper home. Ally is living through hell. No one's day has been good."

"What about Luke?" Harper asked, smiling when Jared shoveled food on her plate before tackling his own. "You're so chivalrous," she teased. "You're starving and yet you're worried about me instead of yourself."

Jared merely shrugged. "You've had a long day, too."

"There's plenty to go around," Zander supplied. "I put everything in the slow cooker this afternoon, thinking we would be able to eat it when we found Zoe. It was between searches and I left to look again. I guess it's a different kind of comfort meal now."

"It's exactly what the doctor ordered." Jared offered Zander a heartfelt smile. They didn't always get along, but they were both good men who recognized when to support one another. "Thanks a lot for this."

"Just think, when you move across the street, you're going to miss out on meals like this. Maybe you should've thought about that before you stole my best friend."

Jared's smile slipped. "Are you seriously going to start in on that again?"

"No." Zander made a face. "I was simply messing with you."

"You're good at that."

"I'm the king of that," Zander agreed. "Tell us about Luke, though. I'm guessing that wasn't the most comfortable of conversations."

"That guy is a complete and total ... jerk," Jared replied, opting for a much softer word than he was originally envisioning. "I don't know how he can live with himself."

"I take it he didn't know anything about Zoe's disappearance," Harper noted.

"Nope, and he didn't seem all that concerned. He said he doesn't have anything to do with the kid and he came to an arrangement with Ally, so he doesn't owe child support. He claims he has no motive. Technically, he's right. He did allow us to search his home, although he wasn't happy about it."

"Obviously you didn't find anything," Shawn said. "Was he at all sorry about not being part of Zoe's life? I mean ... I can't imagine having a child out there, my own flesh and blood, living in the same town and never interacting with her.

"I've seen that little girl before and she's adorable," he continued. "She was with her mother a few days ago on Main Street. She had hot chocolate and it was all over her mouth, and when she smiled at me she looked so cute I wanted to buy her more chocolate."

"She's definitely a cutie," Zander agreed. "At the Halloween festival, she insisted on being a princess even though I told her princesses aren't scary. She said she was going to be the first scary princess and that I was allowed to be her prince if I promised to be a scary prince."

Harper's heart plummeted at the memory. "Yeah. She loved you, said you were handsome and definitely prince material."

Zander snickered. "We have to find her. I can't lose a member of my fan club."

"We're going to, but I don't know that I believe Luke is at the center of this," Jared said. "I mean ... the guy isn't perfect. I would never say he is, but he seemed legitimately shaken when I told him what was going on."

"Not shaken enough to rush out and look for his kid," Zander muttered, bitter.

"No, not shaken enough for that," Jared conceded. "He was hard to read, though. His place was full of empty pizza boxes and beer bottles. He didn't exactly act as if he was living a great life."

"Did he tell you anything of note?" Harper queried.

"Just that he was dating a woman named Jessica Hayden until recently. He broke up with her out of the blue, and was apparently rude while doing it. I think that's his normal mode of operation, though. Do you know her?"

Harper nodded. "She's a crisis counselor."

"Yeah. I met her a few weeks ago when that girl died at the school, although I don't really remember her. We stopped by her house hoping to interview her after we finished with Luke, but she wasn't home."

"Do you think she's a legitimate suspect?" Shawn asked. "I mean ... are you thinking that maybe she took the kid as payback for him breaking up with her?"

"That would be a radical form of punishment," Jared countered. "I've heard of weirder things, though."

"What about dogs?" Zander asked. "Why hasn't the state police sent dogs?"

"They did right before dusk. They searched the entire town. It was difficult because the atmosphere was roiled up thanks to all the searchers, but they didn't have to go far.

"The dogs made it exactly one block down the street, to the closest intersection, and then they lost her scent," he continued. "To me, that seems to indicate she got in someone's vehicle. She was long gone before her mother even noticed she was missing."

"If she got in a vehicle, that means she might not still be in town," Harper said. "If it was a crime of opportunity, then whoever took her could be in another city. Heck, it's been long enough for whoever it was to get out of the state."

"True, but I think it was a local."

"Why?"

"Because it took guts to call out to Zoe in the middle of the street when there were so many people around shopping," Jared replied. "Whoever it was understood the rhythm of the town, that people were in the coffee shop ... and the other stores. They knew he or she only had a very small window to operate.

"Plus, you saw the video footage of Zoe," he continued. "While it was difficult to make out her expressions, she didn't look afraid when whoever it was called out and got her attention. Her body language didn't reflect fear."

"What does that mean?" Shawn asked.

"That perhaps she knew her kidnapper."

To Harper, that was almost worse. "Do you think it was planned? I mean ... do you think someone was watching Ally and waiting for an opportunity to lure Zoe away?"

"I don't know. We don't have enough information to make that determination either way."

"What does your gut tell you?"

Jared wasn't sure he wanted to answer the question. He knew if he didn't, though, Harper wouldn't let it go. She was agitated, worked up, and she needed time to decompress. She would only do that if he somehow managed to make her feel better.

"I believe that Zoe is still alive, although I have absolutely no facts to back that up. It's an assumption, and I won't rule out other avenues of investigation because of that assumption."

"Thank you for the clarification, Detective," Zander drawled.

Jared ignored him. "I think whoever took her doesn't plan on harming her. That might be wishful thinking, but it's what I'm holding on to for the time being. I think you should hold on to it, too."

Harper stared at him for a long beat and then nodded. "That's the outcome I want, so I'm choosing to believe that, too."

"Good." He leaned over and gave her a soft kiss. "We'll start from scratch in the morning. Until then, Zander made us a feast and we both need the fuel. I suggest we eat it and get a good night's sleep."

"I've had worse offers."

"I'm holding on to the best offer until we're alone in the bedroom."

Harper brightened. "Fun."

"Only for the two of you," Zander sneered. "It's not fun for me when he's a pervert."

"You'll live."

"Yeah, yeah, yeah."

Five

A solid eight hours of sleep did wonders for Harper's psyche. She was full of hope when she rolled over the next morning and planted a kiss on Jared's stubbled jaw.

"We're going to find her. I can feel it."

Only half awake, Jared cocked an eyebrow and looked down at her pretty face. She was one of those women who didn't need makeup to be beautiful. Her soul shone from within and made her the prettiest woman in the world.

"I don't want you getting your hopes up," he said quietly, hating the way her lips twisted. "I know you want to believe she's okay — and I definitely want to believe she's okay — but blinders aren't a good idea. We have to hope for the best but prepare for the worst."

"No." Harper pulled away from him and slid out of bed. "I won't do that."

"Heart ... ."

"No." She was firm. "I believe Zoe is alive and she's out there waiting for us to find her. I won't entertain the alternative. If you don't like that ... well ... I guess we'll simply have to agree to disagree. It won't be the first time and I very much doubt it will be the last."

"I'm not trying to be a downer."

"I know. It's almost Christmas, though, and I believe in miracles. After all, it was a miracle I found you, the world's most perfect man."

Jared groaned as he slapped his hand over his eyes. "You're just saying that to manipulate me."

"I'm saying that because it's true."

"You know exactly how to get me to agree with you."

"I do," Harper agreed. "Right now, I want you to agree to get in the shower with me. Then I want you to agree to a nice breakfast. After that, I want you to agree to bundle up because it's cold out. As for the rest of the stuff, we'll see how the day goes."

Jared recognized he'd already lost so he merely shrugged. "I guess I can live with that."

"I promise to make the shower worth your while."

"I can definitely live with that."

"Somehow I knew you would say that."

ZANDER AND SHAWN WERE already up and in the kitchen when Harper and Jared joined them forty minutes later. Zander was briskly stirring pancake batter while Shawn grilled sausage links.

Jared's stomach growled in response, causing Harper to laugh.

"You know, things are going to be different when we move into our house. I don't cook. You're going to be stuck with toast and cereal."

"Um ... I'm coming over here for breakfast every morning," Jared countered. "I don't know what you're doing, but my mornings will be exactly the same. The walk from the bedroom to the kitchen will simply be longer."

"And what if you're not invited?" Zander challenged.

"Oh, we both know that's not going to happen. You're going to want Harper over here as often as possible. That means she'll be bringing me with her for breakfast."

"Hey, I might want Zander's world-famous breakfasts all to myself," Harper countered, frowning when she heard her cell phone ring in the other room. "I have to get that in case it's a job I need to turn down — we're looking for Zoe, not ghosts, this holiday season if anyone cares — but I'll be back to finish this argument."

Jared watched her go with a mixture of amusement and adoration. Then he remembered he was in the middle of an argument. "You're going to cook me breakfast and love it."

"You stole my best friend. I'm not cooking for you if I don't have to."

"Oh, geez." Shawn rubbed his forehead. "This is the argument that will kill me. I can feel it. It makes me think I'm like five minutes from an aneurysm."

"Oh, you're such a baby." Zander poked his side. "This is barely an argument."

"He's right," Jared said, amused at Shawn's long-suffering expression. "This is like a mini-argument … or a toddler argument, if you will."

"The fact that you guys have named your arguments bothers me like you wouldn't believe," Shawn groused. "I thought things would get better when we separated into two households. Now I'm starting to wonder if they're going to get worse."

"They won't." Jared was sure of that. "I think we're all going to get along better when we're not on top of each other all the time."

"Puh-leez." Zander rolled his eyes. "You're planning on being on top of Harper twenty-four hours a day once you move. I know how your perverted mind works."

"I think you believe that because your mind is the one that's perverted. In fact … ." Jared lost his train of thought when Harper returned to the room. He could tell right away that something was wrong by her pallor. "What happened? Are you okay?"

Harper nodded as she gripped her hands together in front of her. "I'm fine. Why wouldn't I be fine?" Her voice was much shriller than normal, which caused Zander to tilt his head.

"You're not fine. You haven't been this pale since the time your mother invited you to a spa weekend and you found out you'd be staying in the same room. What's wrong? Wait … is that your mother's gift again this year? If so, you can fake sick to get out of it."

"That wasn't my mother." Harper chose her words carefully. "That was Michael Jordan."

Jared blinked several times in rapid succession. "The basketball player?"

"Please tell me it's the hot actor," Zander countered. "He's all sorts of ... yum, yum."

"While I would normally take offense at you drooling over another man when I'm in the room, I have to agree about Michael B. Jordan," Shawn said. "I'll play boxing games with him every day of the week."

"Michael Jordan the attorney," Harper corrected. "He's Quinn's attorney."

All three men came rushing back to reality.

"What does he want?" Jared asked, abandoning the coffee pot and moving closer to her. "Did he threaten you? Did he try to bribe you? I will have his law license yanked so fast."

"I'll do worse than that," Zander snapped. "I'll kick him in his private parts and make it so he can never have children. I won't even feel a little sorry about it."

"I'll help him," Shawn offered.

Even though she was feeling discombobulated, Harper couldn't stop herself from smiling. "I love the different sorts of backup I always have at my disposal."

"Yes, we're all knights in shining armor," Jared drawled. "Tell me what the attorney wanted. If he's trying to threaten you, I'll handle it."

"He's not threatening me," Harper said hurriedly. "He called to ask me if I'd be willing to stop by the county jail."

"Why?"

"Because Quinn wants to see me."

Zander, Jared, and Shawn exploded at the exact same time.

"I'm not sure that's a good idea," Shawn hedged.

"He tried to kill you, so he can rot," Zander snapped.

"That's not going to happen," Jared boomed, his eyes firing.

Harper took a moment to absorb each reaction. Only Shawn's didn't irritate her.

"I'm fully capable of making my own decision on the matter."

"Oh, really?" Jared's tone was full of challenge. "And what have you decided?"

"I'm not sure yet." Harper averted his gaze and moved to the coffee pot. "How fresh is this?"

"I just made it," Shawn replied, earning a smile from her as she poured a mug.

"That's good. I think I'm going to need a lot of caffeine today." Harper focused on adding sugar and cream to her coffee before risking a glance at Jared and Zander. She found both of them standing shoulder to shoulder, determined looks on their faces. "Oh, good grief. I hate it when you guys actually agree on something. Somehow that's worse for me, and I still can't figure out why."

"I know why," Jared said. "If we both agree, that means you're in the wrong. We outvote you, and you don't like to be outvoted. If we're split, that means you can usually manipulate one of us into your way of thinking."

Harper scowled. "I think you're making me out to be more of a megalomaniac than I really am."

"And I think you're not going."

She sucked in a breath to calm herself. "Jared, you can't stop me from talking to him."

"Why would you possibly want to talk to him? He tried to kill you. Your whole relationship was a lie. He was using you as part of a grift."

As much as the words hurt, Harper had come to grips with them weeks before. She felt no sympathy for Quinn. She simply had a few things she wanted to say to him.

"We didn't get much of a chance to talk when it was going down," she offered, calm. "I was too busy trying to stay alive to say the things I was really feeling."

"And what are you feeling?" Jared asked, adjusting his voice so it didn't threaten to take over the entire room.

"I feel that I need to get a few things off my chest," she replied. "He was an important part of my life for a bit, and then he derailed it by being scummy. He came back to mess with us, with me in particular, and I want to talk to him about that, too.

"I know you don't understand it," she continued, gently reaching out a hand to touch his wrist. "I know you want me to stay far away from him. He's going to be separated from me by security glass, though. He won't be able to touch me."

"That doesn't mean he can't hurt you."

"No, but I'm beyond his reach now." Harper was so earnest it made Jared's teeth ache. "I was beyond his reach when he came back. I felt guilty for never really loving him, but that's long gone now. I'm fine. I'm going to stay fine. I need to do this."

Jared found that all the reasons he wanted her to stay away from Quinn were really his reasons. His fear had teeth and he wanted to bite. That wasn't fair to her, and he knew it. "Okay."

Harper wasn't sure she heard him correctly. "You're good with this?"

"That's not the correct word. I'm not good with it."

"But you're not going to put up a fight."

"No, I'm not going to put up a fight," he confirmed. "You need to do this. I want you to have everything you need." He thought about the upcoming proposal and realized they both needed to put this behind them if they truly expected to move forward. "I want you to be careful and don't fall prey to his machinations. I'll be close if you need me after."

"Oh, see, this is why I love you." She slipped her arms around his neck and hugged him tight. "It's going to be okay. I'm not going to call you, though. You need to find Zoe. That should be your priority."

"You're always going to be my top priority, but I'm going to let you handle this on your own and not get involved for a change. As long as you promise to be careful, I'm going to step back and let you do your thing."

"I promise to be careful. I always am."

Jared's lips curved down. "That is a lie. You're never careful."

"I promise to be careful *this* time."

"You'd better."

"It's going to be okay. Once it's done, other than testifying at his trial, we'll be done with him. To me, that's something to look forward to."

Jared hoped that was truly the case because if anyone could get under Harper's skin, it was Quinn. The man was a manipulator through and through and he was only happy when he was toying with others. Jail would've limited his options, which meant he was probably feeling feisty.

"I'm only a phone call away." He kissed her cheek. "Don't hesitate to call if you need me."

"I'll be okay. Focus on Zoe. She's the one in trouble."

"Yeah. We're heading toward the former girlfriend's house first. It's doubtful she's a suspect, but we have to rule her out."

"I'll join you this afternoon and offer whatever help I can. Hopefully we'll know more by the afternoon."

"That would be a nice development."

JARED WAS STILL SULKING about Harper's plans when he and Mel parked in front of Jessica Hayden's house an hour later. His mood matched the weather, which was stark and chilly.

"I can tell you're going to be a lot of fun today," Mel groused, exiting the vehicle. "Do you want to tell me what you've been muttering over there for the past twenty minutes?"

Jared stomped his feet extra hard against the cold driveway as he joined his partner. "I don't think you're going to care."

"Let me guess, Harper did something to irritate you."

"Not yet, but soon."

"She told you she's going to do something to irritate you?"

"She's going to see Quinn. His lawyer called this morning and he's asking for a sit-down."

"Oh." Mel was legitimately surprised. Harper and Jared's arguments were generally more tiffs than anything else. He often found it amusing when his partner melted down over things Mel would've completely ignored. Of course, Mel had been married for more than two decades. He knew which battles were worth fighting. As far as Quinn was concerned, he couldn't help siding with his partner. That was a battle he would be more than willing to fight if his wife was the one on the receiving end of a similar call.

"Yeah, oh," Jared echoed, grimacing. "I don't think it's a good idea. She thinks it's necessary. I bet you can guess which one of us won that fight."

"He won't be able to touch her," Mel offered pragmatically as they climbed the steps that led to Jessica's front door. "They take safety seriously at the county jail. She'll be perfectly fine."

"Physically, yes. Emotionally, though? He's a user. I'm afraid he's going to get her all worked up."

"She's a big girl. She knows how to handle herself."

"I guess I can see where you land on this particular argument."

"Yes, I land on your side," Mel said, taking his partner by surprise. "I wouldn't want her going either. It's not your decision, though. It's hers. She has a right to see him if she feels it's necessary.

"He haunted her life for years," he continued. "All that pain and guilt she felt was for nothing. If she wants to unload on him, I don't see what the problem is." Instead of waiting for a response, Mel rapped on the door. "Stop being a baby and focus on the case. Harper will be fine. She knows what she's doing."

Jared scowled. "Well, if you're going to be rational."

Mel waited a full two minutes. When no one answered, he knocked again. After the third knock, he moved to the big bay window at the front of the house and shielded his eyes from the glare so he could peer inside. "It looks empty."

"What are you guys doing?" a female voice asked from the neighboring house, causing both men to jolt and look in her direction guiltily. "Mel?"

"Hey, Irma." Mel plastered a fake smile on his face and smiled at the elderly woman watching them with suspicious eyes. If Jared had to guess, she looked to be in her eighties, although still fairly spry. "How are things?"

"Well, I thought I was coming out here to shoot some bad guys," she replied, lifting the handgun she had hidden away in the folds of her skirt. "Now that I know it's cops, I haven't decided on a course of action yet."

Mel's eyes narrowed. "Um ... are you supposed to have that gun?"

"What gun?" Irma was suddenly innocence and light as the gun disappeared into her skirt again. "Can I get you a doughnut and coffee, Detective?"

Jared bit back a grin as Mel glowered at the older woman.

"We don't have time for pleasantries, Irma. We're looking for

Jessica. We need to question her in regard to Zoe Mathers's disappearance."

All trace of mirth disappeared from Irma's face. "I heard about that. It's terrible. I don't know why you would be looking to talk to Jessica, though. She's a good girl and never gets into trouble."

"Yes, well ... she was dating Luke. We simply have to rule her out, and she was his most recent conquest."

"I told her he was a bad choice, but she wouldn't listen. I told her he would break her heart. Guess what ended up happening."

"He broke her heart," Mel finished automatically. "That's what he does."

"Yeah, well ... ." Irma worked her jaw as she got her emotions under control. "As for Jessica, I haven't seen her since yesterday afternoon. She was on her front porch, looked upset, and she took off in that Japanese car of hers."

"Japanese car?" Jared furrowed his brow. "Is that a euphemism for something?"

"It's a Civic," Mel replied. "Irma's husband worked the lines in the Ford plant for forty years. She doesn't believe in buying foreign."

"It's un-American!" she barked.

"Well, that's not really the important thing to argue about right now, is it?" Mel was calm. "We really need to find Jessica. Do you know where she's been working?"

"No. Like I said, she looked upset. She had a big bag and was loading it in the car and then she took off real quick like. I figured she had an appointment."

Something occurred to Jared. "What kind of bag?"

"One of those small suitcase things with the rollers."

"Do you think she was leaving town?"

Irma shrugged. "I'm part of the Neighborhood Watch, not the Neighborhood Busybody Society. I don't ask about other people's business."

"Okay, well, thank you for your time."

"Don't mention it."

"And make sure that gun is registered," Mel called after her.

"What gun? I think you're imagining things."

Six

Harper was ridiculously nervous as she sat in the chair the jail guard indicated. She expected other people to be around during her conversation with Quinn, but the visitation area was eerily quiet. She was thankful for the guard, who didn't look friendly, but she was starting to wonder if she'd made a mistake agreeing to the request.

"He won't be able to throw a chair through the glass, will he?" Harper asked the guard, her nerves taking over. "I saw that on an episode of television once. I really don't want him to jump on me."

The guard furrowed his brow. "Excuse me?"

"The glass." She gestured toward the huge wall of plexiglass. "He can't jump out and try to kill me, can he?"

"Are you expecting him to jump out?"

"I'm the reason he's in here."

"Really?" Suddenly intrigued, the guard turned to face her. "I heard stories about that takedown. Supposedly it happened in a field."

Harper remembered the location of the final fight very well. "Right in front of a haunted scarecrow."

"What?"

She shook her head. There was no way she would be able to

explain things to him in a cognizant manner. "It doesn't matter." She forced a smile. "His lawyer called and said he wanted to see me. I can't figure out why he would possibly want to revisit what happened."

"I can think of a reason."

Before Harper could question the guard further, a loud clanging sound assailed her ears and she jerked her eyes to the left. Quinn, his hands cuffed in front of him, shuffled thanks to shackles on his feet. The orange jumpsuit he was forced to wear washed out his complexion, and his hair was longer than she remembered.

"Hello, Harper," he drawled as he sat across from her. Instead of phones like she'd seen in movies, there was a speaker set at the bottom of the window, so she had no trouble hearing him.

"Hello, Quinn." The nerves she'd been feeling for the better part of two hours suddenly disappeared, and all she was left with was rage. "Is there something specific you want? Your lawyer called and said you wanted to talk to me."

"I do want to talk to you."

"So ... talk."

Quinn's handsome face split into a wide grin that was more obnoxious than pleasant. "Oh, is that any way to talk to the man who held your heart for years?"

Harper rolled her eyes. "You never held my heart, just that spot in my bowel where I keep my guilt."

The guard made a noise that sounded suspiciously like a choked laugh but kept his eyes pointed forward.

"Oh, don't be that way," Quinn wheedled, adopting a whiny tone. "I'm genuinely sorry about what happened. I didn't mean for it to go down that way. I genuinely didn't have a choice, though. I was trying to protect you. That's why I left in the first place."

"Oh, really?" Harper shot him a withering look. "Do you really think I'm going to believe that?"

"It's the truth. Have I ever lied to you?"

"You faked your death. That seems like a big, fat lie to me."

"Yes, but I was protecting you from my enemies." As if putting on a show, Quinn offered up an exaggerated look around the room before leaning closer. "I was a bad man who wanted to change thanks to the love of a good woman. That woman was you."

Harper wanted to smack him with a chair. It was probably good, she internally mused, that she couldn't break through the glass and attack him. She would hate to have her own bunk in this place before all was said and done.

"You know I'm not going to believe that nonsense, right?"

"But it's true." Quinn refused to back down. "I fell in love with you and I wasn't expecting it. I admit, I first started dating you because I thought you would make a nice front. Plus, well, you were always ridiculously hot." He graced her with a flirty wink that caused her stomach to churn.

"I didn't mean to form real feelings, but I did," he continued. "Each day, they grew. I got to know you, and before I realized what was happening, I was head over heels."

He was a good actor. Harper had to give him that. She understood the game he was playing, though, and she had no intention of falling for it. "Quinn ... ."

He barreled forward before she could shut him down. "There were things from my past that I wanted to hide from, push aside. I couldn't, though. People wanted to hurt me, and if they couldn't get their hands on me, I knew they would have no problem going after you. The only thing I could do to keep you safe was to let them think I was dead. It's not as if I wanted to leave you."

"Oh, yeah?" Harper decided to lure him a bit, if only because she wanted to know what sort of nonsense he would lob at her next. "Why would you possibly come back if you were trying to keep me safe? Did you decide you no longer wanted to do that?"

"No. It's just ... I missed you so much. You have no idea the pain I went through, pining for you for years. It hurt every night when I went to sleep."

"Good grief. How much fertilizer are you going to shovel on my feet?" Harper challenged, her temper flaring to life. "Do you think I'm stupid enough to fall for this?"

He mustered an actual tear, which Harper wanted to smack off his face as it slid down his cheek. "I want you to search your heart. You know the truth is there. I'm not your enemy. I was trying to protect you."

"Oh, so you're my hero, are you?"

"I wouldn't use that word. I've done too many horrible things. I wanted to protect you above all else, though."

"You are the worst liar ever," Harper barked, her tone so loud it caused Quinn to jolt. "The fact that you actually think I might fall for this is horrifying. I'm not stupid. I'm also not weak. I'm not going to believe that story no matter how you spin it.

"Now, if you want something specific, it's probably best you tell me before I storm out of here in a huff," she continued. "I'm too old to play games. And, while you may be bored, and this is the highlight of your day, I have a lot of things on my plate."

"Right." Quinn's eyes darkened. "Let me guess, does Romeo have something special planned for you? Another picnic at your new house?"

Harper's heart skipped a beat. "How do you know about the picnics?"

"I watched you when I came back to see what you were doing. I wanted to be sure I could drive a wedge between you and the cop." All pretense of being pleasant fled as Quinn turned down and dirty. "I knew you were dating him before I ever returned. I had people giving me reports on you from time to time. I had no idea you two were as serious as you were until I saw you in action together."

"Don't bother talking about Jared," she warned, her eyes turning to molten blue fire. "If you say one bad thing about him, I'm out of here. I'm not kidding."

"What makes you think I want to say anything bad about him?"

"I've met you. I was there that day in the field. You would've killed me ... and Molly ... and Jared ... and Zander. You wouldn't have even blinked an eye if it meant you would get that money.

"They found it, by the way," she continued, enjoying the way Quinn squirmed in his chair. "You probably haven't heard because they decided not to make a big deal out of it for the news. The bank, of course, took possession of the money, so you don't have to worry about it being out there waiting to be discovered. It's gone."

"You're lying!" Quinn's voice whipped past fury before he could bank it.

"Hey, that will be enough of that." The guard extended a warning finger, the slope of his shoulders telling Harper he meant business. "If you can't control yourself, Jackson, you're going to have to go in time-out. Do you want to go in timeout?"

Harper had no idea what "timeout" meant, but she doubted it was a good thing, especially given where they were sitting. "Just tell me what you want, Quinn. I don't have time for you. There's a missing girl in Whisper Cove. I need to get back so I can rejoin the search."

"Oh, you're still the martyr, aren't you?" Quinn hissed. "Only you would donate your time looking for a missing kid. I mean ... come on."

"See, that's why you couldn't wedge yourself between Jared and me," she said calmly. "You don't understand what it is to feel things. You don't have emotions. You're a sociopath. You can't understand giving of yourself because it's an alien concept to you."

"Oh, geez. Have you been watching old reruns of *Oprah* or something?"

Instead of reacting with anger, Harper merely pressed the heel of her hand to her forehead and sighed. "What is it you want, Quinn?" she pressed. "If you don't tell me, I'll simply leave."

Quinn opened his mouth in such a way Harper was convinced he had something snarky to say. Instead, he adjusted his stance and offered a smile. "I want to talk to you about your testimony."

"Oh, really?" All Harper could hear in her disappointed mind was "I should've seen this coming" over and over again on a loop.

"You're a good person," Quinn said. "You don't want anyone to suffer, and that includes me. If you testify that I was innocent, that there was a mistake, they'll let me off. I promise to never bother you again if you do this one thing for me."

"No."

"Harper, you owe me."

"How do I owe you?"

"You moved on from my death rather quickly. Heck, without a body, you basically moved in with another guy even though you had no idea if I was still out there fighting to get back to you. That was hurtful, my dear."

"Oh, that's rich." Harper shook her head as the reality of what Quinn truly was washed over her. "You're worse than a sociopath. It really doesn't matter, though. I'm not helping you. You're a murderer, and I have no doubt you'll kill again if you get the chance. If you thought you would be able to charm me ... well, I guess you're mistaken."

"If you're not willing to help, why did you bother to come?" Quinn snarled.

"Because I wanted to see the monster in his cage. I'll sleep better at night knowing that you're in here and never getting out."

"You'd better hope that I don't. You're the first one I'll go after if I get out of this hole."

"Well, then I guess I need to tell the truth in my testimony so you don't get out of here, huh?"

"This is your last chance to help me," he hissed. "If you leave now, I'll never forgive you."

"Good. I guess that means we're finally on level footing. It only took years for me to wise up and make sure that happened."

FELICIA HAYDEN SEEMED SURPRISED to find two police detectives standing on her front porch. Still, she didn't as much as question Jared or Mel before ushering them inside.

"It's getting cold out there," she commented, wiping a light dusting of snow from Mel's coat. "I guess it's that time of year, isn't it? Do you want some coffee?"

"That would be nice," Mel said, following Felicia into her cozy kitchen. He waited until she delivered warm mugs of coffee to him and Jared before speaking again. "We have some questions, Felicia."

"I figured as much." The woman cocked her head to the side, considering. "I saw the news about that poor Mathers girl. I'd assumed you would be working on that until you found her. Did something else take precedence?"

"No." Mel shook his head and sipped. The coffee tasted heavenly after a long morning of searching and questioning. "We're still looking for Zoe. In fact, as part of that search, we were trying to talk to Jessica. We haven't been able to track her down, though."

"Jessica?" Felicia wrinkled her nose. "I don't understand."

"She was involved with Luke until recently," Jared started. "We need to ask her a few questions about the dissolution of that relationship."

This time the face Felicia made was right out of a sitcom. "Oh, of course. I should've put that together myself. I knew that dating Luke was going to come back to bite her. Would she listen to me, though? Oh, no. She knew better ... and look what it got her."

"I take it you weren't a fan of the relationship," Mel noted drily.

"I was embarrassed by the relationship is more like it," Felicia replied. "I mean ... Luke Mathers? He's worse than the gum you find stuck to the bottom of your shoe. He's a terrible man. I mean ... a really terrible man."

"How did Jessica and Luke hook up?"

"They met at the gym. Well, I guess they knew each other before that, but just in passing. They worked out together one night and the next thing I knew Jessica was constantly smiling and giggling as she told me about what a great guy he was."

"How long did they date?"

"Several weeks. Thankfully, I didn't have to see them together very often. Jessica was smart enough to keep him away from me."

"Was she worried Luke would be rude?"

"She was worried I would smack him over the head with a golf club. I still have her father's old set laying around because he never took it with him after the divorce. I've been debating what to do with them."

Jared swallowed the mad urge to laugh at the woman's deadpan delivery. Now was not the time.

"What about their breakup?" Mel asked. "My understanding is that Luke dropped the bomb on Jessica with very little notice. He said she was upset but accepted it quickly. Was that your take on the matter, too?"

"She thought she could change him," Felicia explained. "I'm sure that every woman who has taken him on over the past decade thought the same thing, and that includes Ally. None of these women ever learn until they're forced to grapple with his selfishness on their own terms.

"She thought things were going her way right up until he ended things," she continued. "She was so stunned, all she could do is call him a few names before storming out. Because he's the world's biggest jerk, he actually had a box with her stuff — items she left at his house during overnight visits — ready for her. He wanted to make sure she had no reason to come by again. Told her that would make it uncomfortable for her and he was really doing her a favor."

"He sounds like a real prince," Jared supplied. "What about after, though? You said she was surprised and didn't have a chance to react. What about after she settled?"

"She was angry and hurt, although I think she realized she dodged a bullet," Felicia replied. "Things could've been much worse. He could've knocked her up and abandoned her like Ally. He could've given her a venereal disease. The man is not picky when he chooses his partners. Things definitely could've been worse."

"Yes, well .... we still need to find Jessica," Mel pressed. "We need to be able to cross people off our suspect list if we're going to find Zoe."

"Why would she have anything to do with Zoe's disappearance?"

Mel shrugged, noncommittal. "Maybe because Luke dumped her and Zoe is a tangible tie to him. Sure, he hasn't raised her, but he is her biological father. Even he would have no choice but to capitulate to the will of a kidnapper to save that little girl."

"And you think Jessica is capable of kidnapping a three-year-old child?" Felicia was incensed. "I think you should get out of my house."

Mel held up his hands in surrender. "I don't think Jessica had anything to do with it. I have no choice but to formally rule her out, though. We have a missing child. Time is of the essence."

"Well, I don't know where Jessica is," Felicia said. "She's been angry with me since the breakup because I might've been more unsympathetic than she expected regarding her feelings. She'll get over it, though. She's probably moved on to some other guy already. I mean ... I love my daughter, but she has bleeding tragic taste in men."

"When was the last time you talked to her?"

"A few days ago, right after Luke broke up with her. She was a sobbing mess and I told her to suck it up and get over it. I mean ... everyone knew he was going to dump her. That's what he does."

"And you're positive she wouldn't take Zoe, right?" Jared asked, ignoring the anger flitting across the woman's face. "We have to ask. I'm sorry."

"I can guarantee she wouldn't take that kid," Felicia said. "She doesn't even like kids. She never wanted them. She started telling me that when she was ten and I thought it was something she would grow out of, but she never did.

"That's one of the reasons she thought she was such a good match for Luke," she continued. "He didn't want kids; she didn't want kids. That was a romance for the ages in her book. She thought she had a good chance of snaring him for that reason alone."

"And you have no idea where she is?" Mel tried one more time. "We don't want to arrest her, simply rule her out."

"I honestly don't."

Mel wasn't convinced. "Would you tell me if you knew?"

"Probably not, but it doesn't matter. I really don't know."

"Okay, well, if she calls, it's important you get in contact with us. We need to find that little girl. The sooner we can rule out Jessica, the better."

"I'll keep that in mind."

Seven

Harper texted Jared that she was free and clear of the jail and would talk to him about what transpired later. She stressed she was fine, that there was nothing to worry about, and insisted that he focus on work rather than her.

Jared did none of that.

"What do you think happened?" He stared at his phone as Mel navigated through the familiar Whisper Cove streets. "Do you think he tried to get her on his side?"

Mel shot Jared a dumbfounded look that was somewhere between sympathy and frustration. "Seriously? Of course he was trying to get her on his side. He doesn't have a lot of moves to make. If Harper were to change her testimony ... well ... that's pretty much his only option."

"She's not going to do that."

"Of course she's not going to do that. He has to try, though, doesn't he?" Mel pulled into Luke's driveway and killed the engine to his cruiser. "Look, I get why you were upset. Whether you want to admit it, Quinn had a huge impact on your life."

"I wouldn't say *huge*."

"I would. When you came to town, Harper was starting to come around again," Mel said. "She spent a long time focusing on work and Zander — they were essentially each other's worlds — but that changed when you arrived.

"You two have been good for each other," he continued. "Heck, you've been good for Zander, too. I worried he was going to melt down when Harper finally decided to take back her life."

Jared was incredulous. "Where have you been? Zander does nothing but melt down when he doesn't get his way. He's still whining about us moving across the street."

"See, but that's only one of the reasons you've been good for him," Mel said. "Harper and Zander can't live together forever. They're not Bert and Ernie ... or the Golden Girls. Not only did you find a solution that worked for you and Harper, but you found a solution that worked for Zander.

"Of course he's going to stomp his feet and kick up a fuss," he continued. "That's what he does because ... well ... he's a whiner. He'll be fine after the fact, though, and by keeping him close to Harper, you're proving that you understand what's best for both of them."

Jared's sigh was long and dramatic. "And what does that have to do with Quinn calling Harper to visit him?"

"Oh, right." Mel returned to the here and now with a sloppy grin. "Quinn knows that he's in real trouble and his options are so limited that his only shot is trying to lure Harper to his side."

"That's not going to work."

"No, but he has to try something. Otherwise he's going away for the rest of his life."

Jared muttered something unintelligible under his breath. Mel recognized it as a string of curses, which caused him to smile.

"Fine." Jared finally threw up his hands in defeat. "I'm obsessing about nothing. Can we get back to questioning the world's worst father? I can't tell you how happy I am to be spending time with him again."

IT TOOK FIVE KNOCKS for Luke to answer the door, and when he did, it was obvious to both detectives that he'd only heard the noise because they'd been so insistent. His eyes were red-rimmed, dark shadows haunting them, and his face was unusually pale.

"What do you want?" he asked, his temper on full display. "I answered all your questions yesterday. Unless ... did you find her? Where did you find her?"

Mel and Jared exchanged a quick look.

"We haven't found her," Mel said finally. "We need to ask you a few more questions, though. Something interesting has turned up."

Luke frowned but opened the door to allow them entrance. Once in the kitchen, Jared couldn't believe his eyes. There had to be at least eighteen beer bottles strewn throughout the room. It was obvious Luke tied one on the previous night. The question was, why.

"What insightful questions do you want to ask me now?" Luke asked, heading straight for the coffee pot. "Let me guess, you want to search my mother's house in case I've stashed Zoe there. Well, I can guarantee my mother doesn't have her either. She's in Florida already for the winter, and before you ask, she left a month ago. She doesn't have Zoe."

"We already checked on your mother's whereabouts," Mel offered, ignoring the way Luke rolled his eyes. "We're reasonably assured she didn't return to the area to take Zoe."

"Oh, well, if you're reasonably assured ... ."

"We're more interested in Jessica," Mel admitted, watching Luke's face closely for a reaction. "As far as we can tell, no one has seen her since yesterday afternoon. Her neighbor says she left with a bag and hasn't returned and her mother says she hasn't talked to her in days because Jessica was upset over your breakup ... and Felicia basically thought it was funny."

Luke rubbed his chin as he absorbed the information. "I don't know what you want me to say," he said finally. "If you're asking if I think Jessica is capable of taking Zoe, I don't. That's not how she operates. No matter how mad she was, she wouldn't take Zoe."

"Her mother said she never wanted children."

"That's true." Luke bobbed his head. "She thought we'd bonded over that. She assumed that I didn't want children, so she laid it on thick with the kid hate when we were hanging out."

"You know why she assumed you didn't want children, right?"

Luke balked. "What happened with Ally wasn't my fault. She trapped me."

"You probably don't want to go there right now," Mel warned. "People are up in arms about Zoe's disappearance. If you start your nonsense about attacking Ally again, the pitchforks might actually come out."

"Whatever." Luke screwed up his face into a harsh glare. "She knew I wasn't ready and yet she got pregnant anyway. If that's not a trap, I don't know what is."

"We'll have to leave that discussion for another day," Mel said. "Right now, we're focusing on Jessica. She hasn't been to work, although they call her when they need her and only one call has gone unanswered so that doesn't necessarily mean anything. We need to know if there's any place you can think of that Jessica would go to hide."

"No." Luke was earnest. "Listen, I honestly don't think she would do anything to hurt Zoe. What would be the point?"

"Maybe she wants to erase your mistake," Jared suggested, his eyes never leaving Luke's face. "Maybe she thinks getting rid of Zoe will win you back."

"No." Luke vehemently shook his head. "She wouldn't do that. Even if she was angry with me — which she probably is, I won't deny that — she wouldn't hurt Zoe. That's not who she is."

Jared held his gaze for a long beat and then nodded. "Okay. We still need to find her, rule her out. Where would she hang out?"

"If she's not home, I honestly don't know."

"Then think about it. This is important."

THIRTY MINUTES LATER, Luke still had no suggestions on where to look for Jessica. Mel and Jared were no further ahead than they had been when they arrived. They waited until they were back in the cruiser to give voice to their thoughts.

"What do you think?" Mel asked, turning the ignition key.

"I don't know what to think," Jared admitted, holding his hands in front of the vents so he could feel the warmth the second it came. "He's a mess, though. He's not holding together very well."

"What do you mean?"

"He's being eaten alive by guilt. That's why he's drinking the way he is."

"What kind of guilt?" Mel was legitimately intrigued at the prospect. "Is he feeling guilty for not being there when his kid needed him, or guilty because he's done something he can't take back?"

"That is the question," Jared pursed his lips as he stared at the house. "I don't know what to believe. I find it interesting that no one has seen Jessica in twenty-four hours, though. What are the odds she would disappear at the exact same time Zoe was taken? I mean ... that's weird, right?"

"I've known Jessica on and off for a long time," Mel countered. "She's never struck me as unbalanced."

"Fair enough. The thing is, Luke strikes me as the sort of guy who can derange a woman in five seconds flat. Maybe she wasn't unbalanced until he broke up with her."

Mel opened his mouth, a denial on the tip of his tongue, and then he changed course. "It's weird that she's suddenly gone. I can't argue with that point. I would feel a lot better if we could find her."

"We need to look elsewhere."

"I'm open to suggestions."

"That's the problem. I have no idea where to start."

HARPER MET ZANDER AT the coffee shop upon leaving the county jail. She knew Zander would melt down if he didn't get an update ... and fast. She was also determined to be involved in the search for Zoe, so it made sense to kill two birds with one stone since the coffee shop had become something of a makeshift command center.

"What's going on, Rose?" Harper asked as she waited for the woman to make her drink. "Any news?"

"I was going to ask you the same thing," Rose replied. "I've seen the state police running all over town with dogs today, but they don't seem to be going far."

"They're probably double-checking yesterday's results."

"Which were?"

Harper wasn't sure she should be spreading police business far and wide, but Jared hadn't admonished her not to tell, so she didn't see the harm in it. "The dogs stopped right in the middle of the intersection. That probably means, whoever it was lured Zoe into a vehicle and then drove off with her."

Rose's expression darkened. "I don't like the sound of that."

"Join the club. Have you seen Mel and Jared yet today?"

Rose shook her head. "No, but I heard they visited Felicia Hayden. She told Jenn Dombrowski that Jessica is wanted for questioning, and she's not happy about it."

"I can't say as I blame her, but a little girl's life is on the line," Harper noted. "She needs to suck it up."

"I agree with you there. I can't picture Jessica as a kidnapper, though."

In truth, neither could Harper. "They're probably trying to eliminate her from the list. Since they don't have an obvious suspect, they have to work backwards instead of forward."

"You know a lot about police business," Rose said, handing over Harper's coffee. "Is that because you're moving in with a police detective?"

Harper shook her head. "No. Zander loves police procedurals."

"Ah, well, he's waiting for you in the corner. Let me know if you find out anything."

"I definitely will."

Harper sidestepped two excitable women as she crossed the shop, joining Zander at the table. She slipped out of her coat and sighed when she realized he'd snagged the table with the heat vent directly underneath it. The spot had been their favorite since they were kids and their mothers brought them in for quick visits.

"You remembered." Harper smiled as she sipped her coffee and kicked her feet over the vent. "Ugh. I want to live here it's so warm."

Zander smirked as he turned his attention to her. "You look okay," he said after a beat, his fingers gentle as they ordered Harper's hair. "I take it Quinn didn't try to emotionally manipulate you too badly."

"Oh, he tried. I simply didn't let him."

"Good for you." He patted her wrist. "Tell me what he wanted, though. I'm dying to hear what kind of scam he tried to run this time."

"I think you're destined for disappointment. He didn't try anything unique. It was a little sad really." Harper told Zander about her morning, leaving nothing out. When she was done, Zander's fury was palpable.

"I can't believe he thought you would simply change your testimony to help him out of the goodness of your heart," Zander seethed, his eyes flashing with malice. "I mean ... what is wrong with him? Did he really think he would be able to charm you into doing his will?"

"I think part of him thought it was well and truly possible," Harper admitted. "The other part, though, well ... that part knew that it simply wasn't going to happen. He invited me there to play games. He's bored and wanted news from the outside world."

"Did you give him any?"

"Other than telling him I was busy and didn't have time for his crap, not really. He called me a martyr because I was looking for Zoe. I pretty much ignored him."

'Do you think you'll go back?"

She shook her head. "No. I said all I wanted to say. I have no interest in listening to him. He's broken, and he has nothing to offer me."

"What did you want him to offer you?"

"Maybe an explanation. Maybe something to explain his actions. I don't know. It sounds weak and ridiculous in hindsight, but I wanted to understand how he could be so evil."

"I don't think he's capable of explaining that."

"No." Harper took another sip of her coffee and scanned the coffee shop. "It looks like the search is continuing with no luck, huh?"

Zander bobbed his head. "Everyone is out looking, although it's not going well. I think we'll be out of places to search by the end of the day."

"She's not hiding behind a dumpster waiting for us to find her," Harper noted. "Someone took her. We need to shift the search parameters."

"Do you have any idea of how to do that?"

"No, but I'm going to give it serious thought."

"Good. I ... ." Zander trailed off, his coffee mug close to his lips, and focused on the door as it opened. Naturally, Harper followed his gaze and found Shana striding into the shop. She looked tired, as if she'd been up late into the evening, but her shoulders were broad as she headed toward the counter.

"Rose said that Ally left with Shana last night," Zander volunteered. "I'm guessing that Shana took care of her, which is pretty nice considering everything Shana has been through."

"Maybe situations like this bond people," Harper mused, her mind busy. "Maybe, once you've been through a legitimate trauma, you really do have insight on how to help people."

"Maybe." Zander didn't look convinced, but since Shana was heading in their direction, he had no choice but to paste a bright smile on his face as she approached. "Hello. We were just talking about you."

"Really?" Shana arched an eyebrow. "What were you saying? Good things, I hope. I like hearing good things about myself."

"We heard you took Ally home last night," Harper volunteered quickly. "That was very nice of you, especially since no one else could figure out what to do with her given the circumstances."

"Well, that's not exactly true," Shana hedged. "I took her home. To *her* home, I mean. I sat with her, waited until she fell asleep, and then slept on the couch. I figured she shouldn't wake up alone."

"Given the circumstances, I would agree with that." Harper sipped again, something occurring to her. "Was Ally better this morning? I know Jared and Mel need to question her, so it would be really helpful if she was feeling better."

"She's still a mess," Shana replied. "I think she'll grow stronger as the day progresses, but it's going to take some effort. I decided to give her a break and a bit of time alone, which is why I'm here. I also wanted to find Jared and Mel. When I saw you, I thought perhaps you were expecting them to meet you."

"I believe they're busy elsewhere," Harper said. "Is there something specific you need from them?"

"Actually, there's something I want to share with them." Shana glanced over her shoulder to make sure no one was listening and then lowered her voice to a conspiratorial whisper. "I heard gossip on the street on my way here, and someone said there was a van with dogs painted on it in the intersection close to the time that Zoe disappeared yesterday."

Harper was taken aback by the conversation shift. "A van with dogs on it?"

"Yeah, like a white van, but it had cute puppies painted on it," Shana replied. "If you ask me, that seems like a weird thing to paint on your van."

"I would agree with that," Harper said. "Unless ... well, I guess the van could belong to a mobile veterinarian or something."

"I don't know about that." Shana held her hands up in mock surrender. "I don't want to get anyone in trouble. It's just ... I think it's important for the police to look everywhere. If they overlook something, they might regret it later. I know all about regret. It's not fun."

Harper instinctively nodded, her heart constricting at the way Shana said the words. "I definitely agree with that. I'll call Jared right away and make sure he has the information. Do you know anything else about the van?"

Shana shook her head. "Just that it was white with either decals or a custom paint job. I'm sure it can't be hard to find."

"That would be my guess, too."

"Thank you for relaying the information to the police for me."

"No problem. I ... ." Harper didn't get a chance to finish what she was saying because Shana had already turned on her heel and moved to the other side of the shop and was already engaging in a new conversation. "Apparently she found people who were more interesting than us, huh?"

Zander snickered. "No one is more interesting than us, Harp."

"What do you think about the van story?"

"I think that a van with puppies on it would be a good way to entice kids."

Unfortunately for Harper, she felt the same way. "Yeah. I need to call Jared. It might be nothing but … ."

"It might be the break we needed," Zander finished. "Definitely call him. It couldn't hurt."

Eight

Harper called Jared right away, which was a relief to his continually expanding emotional upheaval. Instead of explaining the information she had over the phone, he insisted on coming to her. He assumed she needed to talk about what happened with Quinn. So, when she immediately launched into Shana's van story, he was understandably confused.

"Wait ... what?"

"There was a van with puppies on it?" Mel asked, furrowing his brow. "That doesn't sound normal."

"Not even remotely normal," Zander agreed. "I think that a puppy van would be the ideal vehicle for snagging children because ... who doesn't love a puppy?"

Harper slid him a sidelong look. "I wanted to get a dog years ago and you said no."

"That's because they're dirty and we work too much to have a dog."

"We could've taken the dog with us to the office so it was never alone."

"That doesn't solve the dirty issue."

"Whatever." Harper rolled her eyes until they landed on Jared. "Can you believe this guy? You're open to getting a dog one day, right?"

"I don't see why not, but I would prefer we talk about it when we have time to sit down and really hammer out the issues," Jared replied. "I don't want this to turn into a thing where *we* get a dog and *I* end up taking care of it."

Harper balked. "I would be an excellent pet owner."

"Then I'm sure it will work out." Instinctively, Jared stroked her hair. "Are you okay after what happened at the jail this morning?"

Harper's sea-blue eyes widened. "Of course. Is that why you thought I called? I'm perfectly fine, Jared. Nothing bad happened."

"What did happen?"

"We can talk about it later. It's not important now."

"I think you should at least give him a hint," Mel interjected. "He's been a whiny baby all morning because he's been worried about you."

Harper studied Jared's strong profile for a long beat and then acquiesced. "Fine. It was nothing. He wanted me to change my testimony and he promised that he would leave and never come back if I did. I told him that wasn't going to happen and I was looking forward to him spending the rest of his life in prison."

"That's it?" Jared was dubious. "That's all he wanted?"

"Well, his initial approach was to claim he got involved with me as a cover but then fell in love with me," she admitted. "It was kind of like a bad romance novel. He couldn't keep up the facade long, though, and when I called him on it he let his true colors show."

"He didn't hurt you, did he?"

"No. We were separated by glass and there was a guard on my side of the window, as well as his. He didn't do anything but cry like a little girl."

"I wish you would've taped it," Zander muttered, his expression turning dark. "We could've uploaded it to YouTube and had a grand time."

Harper patted his hand. "Next time."

Despite himself, Jared smiled at the interaction. If Harper was putting on an act, it was a good one. She seemed genuinely relaxed and happy, eager to get to work on finding Zoe. That was a much better outcome than he envisioned. "Well, as long as you're okay, we're going to start looking for this van. I don't know that it will lead anywhere, but it can't hurt to try."

"Good luck on that," Harper said. "Zander and I are going to hit a few lesser-known places and look for Zoe. We know she's probably not there, but at least we can say we looked. We don't have anything else going on."

"That sounds like a plan." Jared gave her a quick kiss. "I'll see you for dinner tonight, right?"

"The Christmas festival is downtown tonight," Harper reminded him. "I'm guessing it's going to become something of a candlelight vigil given what's going on, but there will be food at the festival."

"And good food," Zander added. "They have these mini pumpkin pies that are to die for. I wish someone would share the recipe, but alas, it's apparently a secret that Rose is going to take to the grave."

Jared chuckled. "Festival it is. I'll be in touch. You guys be safe while you're out and about."

"You don't have to worry about us," Harper said. "Worry about Zoe. She's the one who is in trouble."

"That's why we're tracking down the van. I'll let you know if I find anything."

"You do that."

FINDING A VAN WITH DOGS painted on the side turned out to be harder than it sounded. Finally, Mel did the unthinkable and called his busybody wife to see if she knew who the van belonged to, which seemed doubtful. To his utter surprise, she offered a name right away.

"Edwin Partlow."

"Excuse me?" Jared raised his eyebrows. "Who is that?"

"He's supposedly the guy with the van," Mel said as he disconnected his phone.

"Your wife actually knew?"

"You would be surprised at the odd and strange things my wife knows."

"Apparently so." Jared typed the name in on his computer and frowned as he searched the records. "He lives on Pleasant Ridge Road."

"That's isolated out there," Mel noted, shuffling closer to Jared's desk. "The neighbors aren't on top of one another. If he took Zoe, he could've easily gotten her into the house without anyone noticing."

"Yeah." Jared scanned further down in the file. "He's a sex offender."

Mel's blood ran cold. "You're kidding." What had been a lark a few moments before, a far-off possibility, now became more than that. "What's his level?"

"Level one."

"That doesn't necessarily mean anything," Mel said after a beat. "He might've been assessed as low risk to repeat because of his age or something. Can you get into his file?"

"No. It's sealed, which means he was a juvenile when he committed the crime."

Their eyes locked as they slowly got to their feet.

"We should head out there and have a talk with him," Jared said. "We have to be sure. Even if he's not guilty, if someone did really see him in the area yesterday afternoon, maybe he witnessed something helpful."

"Good point. Let's get on it."

HARPER AND ZANDER SPENT AN hour re-visiting childhood haunts, including visiting the river by their house just in case Zoe was drawn by the water. They came up empty, which was ultimately a relief. Not knowing was terrible, but in this particular case, finding a body would be worse than wondering. Harper had no doubt about that.

With nothing better to do, Harper decided to play a hunch and visit Ally. It felt invasive, as if she was intruding on the woman's grief, but she had to at least try and get information from the traumatized mother. If the van turned out to be a dead end, they needed a place to look.

Ally was forlorn when she answered the door, all traces of energy and life missing from her features. She seemed broken, as if the world had started kicking her and refused to let up. She blinked several times when she realized who was on her porch, and then disappeared inside — leaving the door open — before offering a half-hearted greeting.

"I guess you can come in."

Harper and Zander exchanged a long look, a myriad of emotions passing between them, and then they disappeared inside. This obviously wasn't going to be a comfortable visit, but they had no choice but to push forward.

"How are you doing, Ally?" Harper asked as she followed the woman into a messy living room. There were toys from one end to the other, a pink blanket on the couch, and a stuffed bear that looked like he'd seen better days resting on the coffee table.

"How do you think I'm doing?" Ally asked as she grabbed the bear and threw herself on the couch. "My daughter is missing. My life ... is over."

"Don't say that," Harper chided, moving to the couch. Even though there were items strewn in every direction — clothes, coloring books, dolls, and dress-up clothes — she did her best to ignore the mess and sat. Zander, on the other hand, was so appalled he decided to stand in the corner and pretend his head wasn't threatening to implode due to the overwhelming urge to clean.

"You don't understand," Ally said, gripping the bear tighter. "She's gone. I wasn't paying attention, and she's gone. This is my fault. I deserve this."

Harper's heart rolled. "You most certainly don't deserve this. You didn't cause this, Ally. It's just one of those things."

"I should've made her stay with me." Ally steadfastly avoided eye contact, which Harper recognized as a way to distance herself from her guests. "She doesn't like being around too many people at once and I thought she would kick up a fuss. That shouldn't have mattered, though. I should've kept her with me."

"That will be enough of that," Zander announced, taking everyone by surprise when he pushed away from the wall and strode toward Ally. "You're her mother. You're not doing anyone any good wallowing like this. You've got to snap out of it."

Hurt flashed hard and fast across Ally's face. "You don't know how I feel."

"I don't," he agreed, bobbing his head. "I have no idea what you're feeling. I assume it must be crippling doubt for you to be acting this way. The thing is, now is not the time for you to fall apart. If ever you needed to be strong, this is it. Zoe is out there, waiting for you."

Ally's lower lip began trembling. "It's all my fault."

"Then make it up to her." Zander refused to back down, instead sitting on the coffee table so he could stare directly into Ally's eyes. He didn't give her an option to look away. "You need to pull it together, because everyone else is out looking for your daughter.

"The state police are in town with dogs," he continued. "Search parties are all over town, looking in every nook and cranny. Jared and Mel are tracking down a van someone saw close to the intersection yesterday afternoon.

"Everyone else is working themselves to the bone to find your daughter and you're being a defeatist," he said. "It's as if you've already resigned yourself to the fact that she's not coming back. You can't think that way. You have to be strong for Zoe. You're her mother. That's your job."

Surprisingly, instead of falling apart further, Ally straightened a bit. "You think I'm being weak, don't you?"

"I think you've taken a hard blow," Zander clarified. "I think you've been through more than any one person should ever have to go through. You've been hit not once, but twice. The first time was when Luke turned on you and abandoned Zoe. The second time is now. You made it through the first time. That means you can make it through the second time."

"Do you think?"

"I know you can." Zander was firm. "Sitting around and feeling sorry for yourself isn't going to help matters, though. You need to get up, get showered, and then join in the efforts to find Zoe. Don't give up until there's absolutely nothing left to fight for. We're certainly not there yet."

Ally stared into his eyes for a long time. Finally, she slowly got to her feet. "You're right. I'm being an idiot. I let Shana kill the hope I was building and that was a mistake. I don't know why I let her tell me how to feel."

"That's the spirit." Zander beamed, and then sobered. "Wait ... what did Shana say to you?"

"That it's easier to let go of hope sometimes. She said she had hope with Chloe, but each year that passed the hope was eroded until it became a little ball of fury in the pit of her stomach and that ball of fury hurt more than the wondering and hoping. Then she joined a support group – and that's why she came to see me because support is important – and that's how she moved on."

Anger flared to life in Harper. "Listen, no one is saying that Shana hasn't had it rough. What happened to Chloe was terrible. She shouldn't be saying things like that to you, though. That's not fair."

"What if she's right, though? She would know better, wouldn't she?"

"I think they're vastly different scenarios," Harper said, choosing her words carefully. "Chloe was older, and probably taken by someone with a specific agenda. Zoe is younger. There's every possibility that someone who is desperate for a child to love simply took her because of the holiday season. We simply don't know yet."

"I guess." Ally ran a hand through her messy hair and exhaled heavily. "I should probably take a shower, right?"

"Definitely," Zander answered immediately. "While you're doing that, we'll tackle the house. It needs a bit of a spruce."

"Don't throw anything away. I mean ... Zoe is going to want her stuff when she gets home."

"We won't throw anything away," Harper promised. "We're simply going to put it where it belongs. Take a shower, put yourself together, we'll come up with a plan after that."

"Okay. I ... okay." She offered up a watery smile. "Thank you. I don't want to give up hope yet."

"Then don't. We all have hope this is going to work out. We need to work together to ensure it."

EDWIN DIDN'T RUN WHEN he saw a police cruiser in his

driveway. Instead, he stood on his front porch, arms crossed, and stared at the interlopers.

"Can I help you, officers?"

"We need to ask you a few questions, Edwin," Mel replied as he warily walked up the driveway. Edwin didn't appear as if he was about to become aggressive, but Mel had been on the job long enough to recognize that things could shift quickly.

"About what?" Edwin queried. "If my neighbor is complaining about the noise again, I apologized. I didn't realize she could hear the music that far away. I've been good since the initial complaint."

"We're not here about the music," Mel replied. "We're here about Zoe Mathers."

Edwin didn't look panicked, instead shrugging his shoulders. "I don't know who that is. Is she a neighbor, too?"

"No, she's the little girl who went missing in town yesterday."

"And you're here to talk to me about that?" Edwin's eyes went wide. "I ... why? I didn't have anything to do with that. If someone said otherwise, they're lying."

"Someone saw your van downtown yesterday," Jared offered. "We're trying to tie off loose ends. Can you tell us what you were doing down there?"

"Sure. As soon as you tell me why you would possibly consider me a suspect in the kidnapping of a kid I've never met."

"Like I said, we're trying to tie off loose ends."

"Uh-huh." Edwin didn't look convinced. "I deliver furniture for the Thompsons out on the highway."

"The ones who make the Amish furniture?" Mel asked.

Edwin nodded. "They're not technically Amish, but they prefer someone else make the deliveries. It works out well for all concerned because I can't make furniture."

Jared slid his eyes to the van in question. "And the reason for the dogs on the van?"

"What? You don't like dogs?"

Jared waited, his eyes never leaving the man's face. He was waiting for him to bolt, although Edwin's relaxed body language pointed toward the opposite.

"I also help with the mobile vet," Edwin said after a beat. "I help with animal rescues and adoptions. The van is merely an advertising tool."

"There's no website on it, though," Mel pointed out. "How is it advertising if people don't know who you represent?"

"The lettering for the mobile rescue was wrong so they had to re-order it. It's due to arrive Tuesday. If you don't believe me, Darcy at the clinic can vouch for me. Is that all?"

"Just one more thing." Jared took a determined step forward. "You're a level-one sex offender. Can you offer us any insight into the charges levied against you?"

Understanding dawned on Edwin's face, and instead of being upset he barked out a laugh. "Oh, that's why you're here. I couldn't figure it out. That charge is from when I was a teenager. I had to register as a sex offender, even though there was nothing sexual about what happened."

"We'd still like to hear it," Mel pressed.

"I urinated on the library wall while drunk with friends during my senior year of high school. The mayor happened to see me, and instead of apologizing, I was a moron and mouthed off. The mayor decided to make an example of me ... and here we are."

"Why not get that expunged?" Jared asked.

"Because getting a sex offense expunged is virtually impossible," Mel answered. "That's why the record was sealed. That's the best the court can do in the current climate."

"Pretty much," Edwin agreed. "You might not like me — and I don't blame you if you don't — but I'm not a kidnapper. I can promise you that."

"You were downtown, though," Jared noted. "Did you see anyone out of place while you were down there? The little girl was in front of the coffee shop. She had on a pink coat and hat."

"I don't think I saw anything out of the ordinary, but I wasn't really looking," Edwin said. "I'm sorry. I can't imagine what that poor mother is going through. There were people on the streets when I was stopped at the intersection, people shopping. I think you were down there shopping." He inclined his chin in Jared's direction. "I only remember because you were with that really loud guy who is always in the gym."

"Zander," Jared supplied helpfully for Mel. "I was with Zander ... and he's right. I was down there."

"I didn't see a little girl," Edwin said. "If I did, I would've told you. I might not be a perfect man, but I wouldn't stand by and let a kid be kidnapped and not do anything about it. That's not who I am."

"Okay, well ... I don't suppose you'd let us search your house just to mark you off the list, would you?" Mel asked. "It would be helpful."

"Knock yourself out. I have nothing to hide."

Nine

Harper dressed warmly for the Christmas festival, opting for her blue parka and a matching hat. Even though electric warmers were moved to Main Street, it was Michigan, and winter in the Great Lakes state meant cold weather.

Jared texted that he would meet her there, so she rode with Shawn and Zander. This was Shawn's first Christmas festival in Whisper Cove, so he had no idea what to expect.

"Is there outside square dancing?"

Zander was insulted by the question. "Do I look like I square dance?"

Shawn took a moment to study Zander's bright red coat and matching boots. "I'm not going to lie. You look like you could do some square dancing if you put your mind to it."

Zander scowled. "I can't believe we're dating."

"That makes three of us," Harper offered as she walked next to Zander. "I thought for sure you would find something to dislike about him by now. Too bad he doesn't have overgrown toenails or nose hairs that you could braid, huh, Zander?"

"Oh, you're so funny." Zander poked her side as Shawn laughed. His reputation with men before Shawn was the stuff of legends and involved freaking out over back hair and climbing out a window to avoid having to explain exactly why the relationship wasn't going to work. Shawn appeared at the exact right time — when Harper and Jared were making plans for the future — and Harper couldn't help wondering if it was destiny, that perhaps Zander stayed single for as long as he did because he knew she needed him.

"I think I am funny," Harper said, slowing her pace so she could study the festival as it popped into view. "It looks fairly normal."

"Were you expecting it to change after thirty years of the same thing?" Zander queried. "I can't ever remember it being different."

"No, but with Zoe missing ... ." She trailed off, not wanting to throw a wet blanket over the festivities.

"They're having a candlelight vigil for her," Shawn volunteered. "I heard people talking about it in the gym today. I think people were upset over what happened to the point where they were considering not attending, but I think that would be a shame."

"Why is that?" Harper was legitimately curious.

"Because this community is coming together to find that girl. The festival is just another way for them to come together. When we find her, Zoe is going to be able to look back on this and realize exactly how many people worked as a group to find her."

"Oh, that's a nice way of looking at it," Harper enthused. "You have a good heart, Shawn. That's only one of the things I love about you."

"I'm guessing you also love me because I regularly take Zander off your hands."

"That, too." Harper giggled when Zander swiped at her, easily sidestepping him and almost crashing into an approaching figure. She had an apology on her lips — she hadn't even imbibed any of the peppermint hot chocolate yet, so there was no reason to be unsure on her feet — but it died when she realized Jared was the one invading her personal space. "Hello, handsome."

Jared grinned as he slipped his arm around her waist and gave her a quick kiss. "Hello, beautiful. You're in a good mood this evening."

"It's Christmas," she said simply. "Halloween is my favorite holiday, but there's still something magical about Christmas."

"You're just looking forward to the spiked hot chocolate," Zander countered.

"That, too. You definitely have to try to the hot chocolate, Shawn. You'll dream about it for the rest of the year. You, too, Jared."

"As lovely as that sounds, I believe I'm going to pass this evening," Jared said. "We need to watch the crowd fairly closely, and I don't think being drunk is going to help that endeavor."

Harper sobered. "Do you think whoever took Zoe is going to be here?"

Jared held his hands palms out and shrugged. "I have no idea. It's a possibility, though. They're having a candlelight vigil. If you don't want to be considered a suspect, the smart thing to do is attend."

"Except you're going to be watching the attendees," Harper pointed out.

"I am, but it's human nature to pretend to be innocent."

"What does that mean for Zoe?" Shawn asked. "If her kidnapper is here, where will she be?"

"I don't know the answer to that either." Jared turned rueful. "We don't know the kidnapper will be here. We have to watch, though. It's all we have."

"I'm guessing the van turned out to be nothing, huh?" Harper asked.

"It did. He let us in his house and there's a legitimate reason for the dogs. He is a sex offender, but it's one of those things that should've never made it on the list."

"Like what?" Zander asked curiously. "Are you talking about whacking off in public or something? Because, if so, I totally agree that's not a crime. It's gauche, but not a crime."

Harper scowled as Shawn choked on a laugh. "That is so gross."

"It's definitely gross," Jared agreed, slinging an arm over Harper's shoulders. "That's not what he was nailed for. It was public urination."

"Oh." Harper made a face. "That's ... weird. I didn't know that was a thing you could get arrested for."

"It's been known to happen a time or two." Jared pressed his lips to her temple, enjoying the way she snuggled in at his side. "So, I was thinking we would get some dinner together and look around before the vigil. We have a little time before that happens, though. Let's spend it together."

"You read my mind."

"There's no reason you can't have the hot chocolate either, just because I can't."

"Oh, don't worry. I'm totally having the hot chocolate. I can't miss that."

"I would say she's exaggerating about the hot chocolate, but she's really not," Zander said. "It is the best thing ever made."

"Then let's get my girl giddy," Jared suggested. "It will be fun since you're going to have to be the one babysitting her during the vigil."

"Oh, I see how your mind works." Zander's expression darkened. "I'm going to pay you back for that when you're least expecting it."

"Bring it on."

THE FESTIVAL WAS AS FUN as Harper and Zander remembered, although they had nostalgia fueling them. Jared and Shawn were amused more than anything else, especially when two high school students walked by with shovels. They were complaining loudly to anyone who would listen, and Jared couldn't stop grinning at their backs.

"What's their deal?"

"Someone has to pick up the reindeer droppings," Harper explained, snickering as the boys headed toward the end of the street. "Santa is down there to meet with the kids, and you can't have Santa without reindeer."

"Santa, huh? Do you want to sit on his lap and tell him what you want for Christmas?"

"I think I'll stick to sitting on your lap."

"Good choice."

They got plates of food from one of the open restaurants and sat at a picnic table close to the warmers. Jared couldn't remember ever seeing the town bustling with so much activity.

"This must be a big deal, huh?" He sawed into his kielbasa as he watched the happy people greeting one another. "I think everyone in town is here."

"Pretty much," Harper agreed, shoveling kielbasa and sauerkraut into her mouth. "Oh, this is marvelous. I only eat this once a year and it's as amazing as it always is. I love it."

"It's pretty good," Jared agreed, his eyes busy as they bounced between faces. He was making a big show of being interested in the conversation, but it was obvious that his mind was on other things.

"Why don't you tell us what you're thinking?" Harper suggested, opting to tackle the elephant in the room. "You can't shut it off. Maybe we'll be able to help."

"I'm thinking that people would notice if someone missed the festival," Jared replied honestly. "I mean ... I don't think everyone would obviously notice, but if someone from your particular peer group was absent, you'd probably question that, right?"

"I would think so," Zander confirmed. "My entire family is here. They're down that way." He jerked his head to point. "Even though I came with Harper and Shawn, if I don't stop to see them, I'll be in big trouble. It's a community event, but it's the one time of the year when everyone treats each other like family."

"So, I wonder who is missing," Jared mused.

"I thought you said that the kidnapper is probably here," Harper argued. "Are you changing your mind?"

"Maybe." He stroked his chin, intent. "There are a lot of people here, more than I imagined. Maybe our culprit wouldn't feel comfortable with this many people around at one time. Or maybe I'm just making this more difficult than I have to."

Harper patted his hand, sympathetic. "I get it. The longer we go without finding Zoe, the more worried you get. You're doing everything you can do."

"Yeah, it's not enough, though. Most missing children are found in the first twenty-four hours. The odds grow staggeringly lower after that. With each passing hour now, it becomes more and more difficult."

"You can't give up."

Jared forced a smile as he turned back to her. "I'm not giving up. If

I've learned anything from falling in love with you, it's that miracles are possible."

Harper went gooey all over as Zander mimed gagging.

"That was the schmaltziest thing I've ever heard," Zander complained.

"Get used to it," Jared ordered, leaning closer to Harper and pressing a kiss to her cheek. "I'm going to keep it up for a very long time."

JARED LEFT HARPER WITH Zander and Shawn so he could join Mel at the fringe of the crowd. The older police detective sipped coffee as Jared sidled up, and almost looked amused when he leaned forward to sniff the cup.

"Are you worried I'm partaking in the peppermint hot chocolate?"

Jared shrugged. "From what I hear, it's practically magical. How can you refrain?"

"You jest, but it *is* downright magical. You have no idea how much I love that hot chocolate."

"Probably not as much as Harper. I think she's already had two mugs, and maybe she snuck in a third when I wasn't looking. I can't be sure."

"That should make her downright lovable by the time you can take her home."

"She's always downright lovable."

"Ugh. You guys are sick. I can't wait until you propose and put me out of my misery. Only men thinking about getting married are as ridiculous as you. Once you're married, you'll realize that romance is a myth."

"Hey!" Jared extended a warning finger and glanced around before continuing. "Don't say that so loud. You're going to ruin the surprise."

"If you would get it over with, there would be nothing to ruin."

"It needs to be a big deal."

"See, I think you're being bamboozled by television and movies to believe that. I proposed to my wife over a bucket of KFC and warm biscuits. She still talks about the proposal."

"I'm guessing it's not in a good way," Jared said drily.

"We're still married."

"And it's a great accomplishment," Jared agreed. "I'm going to have a great marriage *and* proposal. You can have both."

"Fine." Mel held his hands up in mock defeat. "You do your thing. Just get it over quickly so I don't have to worry about what I say. You know I'm not good with a secret."

"I *do* know that," Jared confirmed. "Zander gets that from you."

"And I think we should start making our way around the crowd," Mel intoned. "If we don't, there's gonna be a fight ... with or without the peppermint hot chocolate."

"Fair enough."

HARPER WATCHED ALLY LIGHT her candle for Zoe with a mixture of pride and sadness. The woman was barely holding it together, and yet she was leaps and bounds ahead of where she'd been earlier in the day. Karen was with her, sort of her de facto wingman, and they kept close to one another as volunteers made the rounds with the candles.

"It's a wonderful outpouring, isn't it?" Shana offered, moving to the spot beside Harper. She already had a candle, although it wasn't lit.

"There are a lot of people here who clearly care about Zoe," Harper agreed, shifting from one foot to the other so she could give Shana a sidelong look. "How are you doing with all that's going on?"

"Are you wondering if this brings back memories of Chloe?"

"I would think it would have to."

"Well, you would be right. The thing is, though, I think about Chloe all the time whether there's a missing child or not. Zoe's disappearance obviously reminds me of what happened, but nothing ever truly stops me from missing her."

A bubble of sympathy took up residence in Harper's chest. "I'm sorry. It must be hard for you at this time of year."

"It's hard for me every time of year. Christmas isn't worse or better. In truth, Chloe's favorite holiday was Thanksgiving. She said it was because turkeys were underappreciated."

Harper smiled because she knew it was expected. "Well ... she sounds like a wonderful girl. I don't really remember her that well. We were a bit younger and the high school kids at that point in time were considered mythical creatures by us middle school losers."

"I think she would've grown up to be a wonderful woman." Shana let loose a long sigh. "Sometimes that's what I think about, how she would've turned out. What kind of mother she would've been, if she would've had a career or opted to be a homemaker. The sky was the limit for my girl, and I like imagining what could have been rather than what was."

"I know you probably don't want to hear this, but you don't know with absolute certainty that Chloe is dead," Harper hedged. "She could be out there somewhere."

"And she purposely stayed away? Why?"

Harper thought of Quinn. "I don't know that I'm the best person to be sharing this conversation with," she said ruefully. "My ex-boyfriend came back from the dead a few weeks ago and tried to kill me. My head is all over the place."

Shana snorted. "I forgot about that. I guess, to you, it's entirely possible for someone to disappear for years and come back, huh? The thing is, I very much doubt it's going to happen twice in the same small town. I know she's gone. I'm a ... realist."

Harper pursed her lips. "I don't want to tell you your business — and I get why it's important for you to be able to put the past behind you and look forward — but you really shouldn't have told Ally to accept that Zoe was gone. We don't know that she's gone yet. There's still a chance we'll find her."

"I didn't tell her she was gone. I said she had to pull herself together and be strong, because whether Zoe is gone or not, Ally is no good to anyone if she curls up in a ball and stops living her life. I certainly didn't mean for her to embrace the fact that Zoe is gone for good. If she took what I said that way ... well, I guess there was some miscommunication."

"I wouldn't worry about it," Harper said, brightening considerably. "Ally is barely on her feet. She might've only heard what she wanted to hear."

"That's true. You wouldn't believe the things I imagined I heard in the weeks surrounding Chloe's disappearance. I thought everyone was saying something they weren't because my nerves were shot, my emotions fragile. It took me forever to crawl out of that hole. I don't want the same thing for Ally."

"None of us want that for her. No one is ready to give up, though. We're going to find Zoe. I have faith … and I want Ally to have it, too."

"There might come a time when she has to give up the fight."

"Maybe. It's not today, though." Harper flashed a small smile before moving to her left. "I need to get a candle and then find Zander and Shawn. It was nice talking to you, Shana. What you're doing for Ally is wonderful. She probably doesn't realize it yet, but she will one day."

"I'll see you around, Harper. I … oh, wait." She screwed up her face, something occurring to her. "Did you ever track down the owner of the van?"

"I didn't, but Jared did. Turns out it was a dead end."

"Oh?" Shana looked disappointed. "I'm sorry to hear that. I was hopeful that would prove to be a vital clue."

"No. It turns out the guy was a sex offender, so they really thought they were getting somewhere, but he was delivering furniture and simply didn't have time to carry out the deed. And, well, he was on the sex offender registry for public indecency, not a sex crime. It's a whole big thing. He's not a suspect, though."

"Well, that's too bad. I hoped he would lead you to Zoe."

"We all did. I'll see you around." Harper offered a half-wave and turned to find Zander and Shawn. She'd barely made it through the crowd, to where she thought they would be standing, when she pulled up short.

There, standing on the far side of the gathering, was a forlorn woman. She had long dark hair and glittering eyes. If Harper didn't know better, she would've assumed she was crying. That was impossible, though, because the woman wasn't there for the candlelight vigil. She was there because she was dead, which meant she had numerous other problems.

"Oh, well, crap," Harper muttered, her heart rolling. "This isn't a Christmas miracle."

Ten

Harper tracked the ghost as she sidled through the crowd, barely paying any attention to the people she crossed paths with as she moved away from the bustling activity.

For her part, the ghost loitered on the other side of the fence that separated the main drag from the park. Harper didn't immediately recognize the woman — and had no reason to believe she had anything to do with Zoe's disappearance — but she couldn't drag her eyes away from the specter.

The ghost didn't look at Harper, instead studying the group of people toward the center of the action. Harper didn't as much as look over her shoulder because she already knew who was standing there. Ally. She was surrounded by the people supporting her and trying to hold it together with all eyes on her.

Harper swallowed hard as she hit the street, took a moment to look both ways, and then turned back to the woman ... only to find her gone. She pulled up short, her heart thumping hard, and scanned the park for signs of movement. Unfortunately, the ghost that had been there only moments before was gone, and there was no indication where she went.

"Harp, what are you doing?" Zander called out, drawing her attention back to the festival. "You need a candle."

"Sorry." Harper forced a smile that didn't make it all the way to her eyes. "I'm coming. I'll be right there."

SNOW WAS FALLING WHEN Harper woke the next morning and instead of bouncing out of bed, she snuggled closer to Jared so she could watch the large flakes slowly drift to the ground through the window. Jared was still out, his eyes closed, but he instinctively slipped his arms around her as she nestled her face against his shoulder.

She couldn't shake the idea that the ghost's timely appearance the night before was important. Of course, she had no idea who the woman was, so it was possible she'd been dead for years and only drawn to the area because of the crowd. Harper had no way of knowing the woman had information ... and yet something inside niggled for her to go back and track down the lost soul.

"I can hear you thinking so loudly that I'm afraid you're going to wake the dead," Jared muttered around a yawn.

Harper tilted her head so she could study his handsome face. "I'm sorry I woke you. It's snowing out. I love snuggling in the snow."

He pried open one eye and smiled. "If I could, I would call in sick and we could snuggle all day. I promise to make it happen before winter is over."

"That sounds fun." She rubbed her cheek against his chest. "Did you see anyone of interest at the vigil last night?"

"Everyone was of interest ... and also boring at the same time, if that makes sense."

Oddly enough, that made perfect sense to Harper. "Everyone could be a suspect, but they also could be innocent."

"Pretty much."

"Huh." She rubbed her hand over his bare chest as he tugged the covers up to cover both of them, drawing them over their heads and causing her to laugh. "What are you doing?"

"I want to live here, in this bed tent, with you for the rest of my life." He kissed her, not caring that he could barely see her in the darkness. "This is a happy place."

"You really are feeling schmaltzy these days, huh?"

"Maybe, or maybe I simply know what I want. Like, right now, I would give up pretty much everything to stay in this bed for the next twelve hours."

"What would we do for food?"

"Make Zander deliver it to us."

"Yes, because that sounds like something he would do."

"Well, I didn't say he would be happy about it." Jared's fingers were gentle as they brushed her hair away from her face. "You haven't told me much about your meeting with Quinn. I'm trying not to push, but if you want to talk, I'm here."

Harper blew out a sigh. "There's nothing much to talk about. He tried to manipulate me and failed. Then he tried to get me to agree to change my testimony and failed again. It's not as if we had some deep and meaningful conversation."

"No? I thought maybe he would apologize for what he did to you."

"I guess, in his roundabout way, he did. He made up stories and tried to tell me things I knew weren't true. I didn't believe him, if that's what you're worried about."

"I'm just worried about you. What happened with Quinn was ... out there. It would only be normal for you to question things after the fact."

"The only thing I'm questioning is how I didn't see him for what he was from the start."

"You were young."

"Yeah, well, young doesn't mean stupid. That's what my dad always says."

"You mean the man who is fighting over an antique cuckoo clock that doesn't even work as he continues to battle it out with your mother in a divorce that has been going on for years?"

Harper sighed. "That would be my one and only father."

Jared chuckled as he wrapped his arms around her slim body, pulling her close as they kissed. "I love you, Harper Harlow."

"I love you, too, Jared Monroe." Her eyes sparkled. "You're acting extremely mushy this morning, though. I find it ... interesting."

"I'm acting romantic," he countered. "Who doesn't love romance?"

"Good point."

They lapsed into amiable silence, the only sound Harper could register coming from Jared's heart as it beat against her ear. Then, suddenly, she remembered something and bolted upright. Since the covers were over her head, she got tangled and had to fight her way free.

"What's wrong?" Jared asked as he joined her in the real world. "I thought we were having a nice moment."

"We were. It's not that. It's just ... I saw a ghost at the candlelight vigil yesterday."

Jared's heart dropped. "And you're just telling me now? Was it Zoe?"

"No." Harper vehemently shook her morning-mussed head. "It wasn't Zoe. It was a woman. She was older. I would say in her late twenties. Part of me thought I should recognize her at the time. The other part wasn't so sure."

Jared blinked several times before speaking. "You recognized her."

"I'm not sure." She chewed on her bottom lip, uncertain. "I don't suppose you have a photograph of Jessica Hayden, do you?"

The question caught Jared off guard. "Are you serious?"

"Yeah. I've only met her once or twice, and we've never been what I would consider close. I think that maybe the ghost I saw was her, although I can't be certain."

"Hold on." Jared slid out of the bed. "I'll be right back." He disappeared through the bedroom door, returning two minutes later with his tablet and climbing under the covers as he booted it up. "It will just take me a second."

"Okay." Harper leaned her head against his shoulder as he worked, and Jared planted a hard kiss in the center of her forehead.

"Here we go," he said after a few keystrokes. "Is this the woman you saw?"

Harper focused on the computer screen, on the pretty brunette with the bright eyes and easy smile. There was a lump in her throat as she slowly nodded. There was no doubt the woman she saw in the park was Jessica. "Yeah."

"Are you absolutely sure?"

"I'm sure."

Jared heaved out a sigh. "I guess that means she's dead and not on the run with Zoe."

"If she did have Zoe, do you think it's possible she's still alive and not alone ... wherever she is? Zoe, I mean. If Jessica took her and is dead ... what does that mean for Zoe?"

Jared recognized what she was saying right away. "I don't know, Heart. I guess we have no choice but to find out, though."

"Definitely."

AN HOUR LATER, HARPER and Jared were bundled up and at the park. Jared left his vehicle on the main road and they entered the property from the spot where Harper saw the ghost the previous evening.

"Right here?" Jared asked, holding out a hand to help Harper over the small fence.

Harper nodded, her eyes keen as she scanned the area. She had a knit cap pulled low over her ears and a pair of fuzzy mittens on so she could more easily take them off if she felt the need to touch something. "Yeah. She was standing right here."

She turned and looked back at the street, which looked normal again. The festival steering committee must have been busy after everyone left the previous evening, Harper internally surmised. There was no evidence the town hosted a party.

"I was right there," Harper explained, pointing. "I caught sight of her and started moving in this direction. The street was shut down to through traffic, so I didn't need to look before crossing the street. I did anyway, and that's when I lost sight of her."

"Well, don't blame yourself." Jared moved his hand over her back and scanned the park. It looked empty, desolate even. For some reason, seeing the vacant swings and merry-go-round caused his heart to ping. He was certain Zoe probably enjoyed hanging out at the park, and the only way she would be able to enjoy it again was if they found her … and soon. "I guess we should look around."

"Yeah." Harper bobbed her head. "I'll take this side of the park. You take the other."

Jared balked. "Why don't we stick together, huh?"

Amused despite herself, Harper had to bite back a grin. "I think you're being a little ridiculous. It's the middle of the day and we're out in the open. Nobody is going to grab me or anything."

"I know. It's just … fine." He heaved out a sigh. "It will be quicker if we split up. Don't go too far, though."

"Trust me. I have no intention of spending one more second out here than is necessary. It's cold … and I don't like being cold."

"Well, if you're a good girl, I'll warm you up later."

They split, Jared heading to the west and Harper the east. There were very few places to hide a body given the time of year. In the summer and fall months, the property was drenched in foliage thanks to flowers, bushes, and leafy trees. Now, it was barren, and there were only so many places to look.

Harper kept her gaze intent on the ground to make sure she didn't miss any clues, and when she finally moved to the area behind the huge slide she and Zander used to love playing on for hours at a time as kids, she pulled up short.

She didn't see the body. Not at first, at least, but a chill swept over her at the exact moment she saw hair fluttering in the breeze. To be fair, she didn't realize it was hair for a full ten seconds. She saw something odd moving, tried to wrap her head around what it was, and only found the answers when she caught sight of a perfectly manicured hand hiding amongst the hair.

"Jared," she called out weakly, rooted to her spot.

He didn't hear her. He was too far away.

She cleared her throat and called out again. "Jared!"

This time his head snapped in her direction and he broke into a run. He was at her side within seconds, and he put an arm across the front of her body to keep her from rushing forward.

"Son of a … ."

"That's exactly what I was thinking," Harper said drily. "I think I need to sit down."

MEL WAS THE FIRST ON the scene, followed closely by the county medical examiner's van. Whisper Cove was too small to have their own coroner, so they had to contract with the county for services. Thankfully, they didn't have to wait long today.

"What do we have?" Allison Ryan, one of four pathologists the county employed, asked as she snapped on a pair of rubber gloves.

"Jessica Hayden," Mel volunteered from his perch close to the woman. He was crouched low so he could look over the body from a fresh vantage point, and he appeared uneasy. "We were looking to question her in the disappearance of Zoe Mathers."

Allison's expression shifted. "I see." She took a long moment to scan the immediate area. "No little girl?"

"No. We've looked. She's not here."

"Well, I guess that's something." Allison carefully slipped her hand into the still-fluttering hair and pressed her fingers against the woman's neck. "Just making sure," she said when Jared shot her an agitated look. "That's part of my job description."

"Do you think we didn't check?"

"No. I still have to check myself. I'm sorry if you don't like that."

"Whatever." He moved his hands to Harper's shoulders and gave them a light rub, which wasn't easy given the size of her heavy parka. "Do you have a cause of death?"

"Are you kidding?" Allison's eyes flashed. "I just got here. I actually have to look at the body before making a determination."

"She was struck in the head," Harper automatically offered. "I'm guessing by that huge rock." She pointed toward a huge stone located about two feet from the body.

"What makes you say that?" Allison asked. "And, oh, who are you?"

"This is Harper Harlow," Jared automatically answered. "She's my girlfriend and she was with me when the discovery was made."

Allison narrowed her eyes. "Since when do police detectives take their girlfriends to murder scenes with them?"

"Harper has a special skill set," Mel interjected. "She's the reason we knew to look in the park in the first place."

"Uh-huh." Allison stared so hard at Harper it made the ghost hunter uncomfortable. "I think I've read stuff about you in the newspaper. You were the one who was almost killed by the guy who came back from the dead, right?"

"What does that have to do with anything?" Jared exploded.

"I'm simply trying to understand what she's doing here."

Harper was too cold to continue playing games. "I can see ghosts," she volunteered, ignoring the wild look in Mel's eyes as he fanned his face behind the medical examiner. "I run a ghost-hunting business where we try to help displaced souls cross over. I saw Jessica's soul last night, although she disappeared quickly. It didn't sit well, so we came back this morning to look for her ... and found this instead."

"I see." Allison flicked her eyes back to the body, moving her hands to the back of Jessica's head before speaking again. "She was definitely struck on the back of the head. I don't know that I can say it was with that rock, though."

"There's blood on the rock," Harper volunteered. "I saw it when we were waiting for you."

"Oh, well, then maybe it is the murder weapon." Allison brightened considerably. "That will save time, huh?"

Harper slid Jared a sidelong look and found him watching her with unreadable eyes. "What?"

"Nothing."

"You obviously have something on your mind."

"I just find you adorable. I like that you're your own person and aren't embarrassed to say whatever comes to your mind."

"Yes, I'm a wonder and a joy," she drawled, rolling her neck and turning to her left when she caught sight of a uniformed officer. "Isn't that David Packer?"

Mel turned to look and nodded. "Yes. We sent him to search the area on the other side of the park for Jessica's vehicle. We're hoping to get lucky there, because otherwise, we have no idea where her car is. That's a loose end I don't like."

"We have a lot more loose ends than that," Jared argued. "None of this makes any sense."

"Well, at least we have another direction to look in." Mel straightened and focused on David. "Anything?"

"We didn't find her car on the access road on the far side of the park," David replied, fighting to catch his breath. "We did find it at the library, though. It was just sitting there, right out in the open."

"Seriously?" Mel started to move. "Show me."

They left Allison to do her thing with the body and hurried to the sidewalk. Whisper Cove wasn't large, and the library was only two blocks away. Harper's heart was pounding as she fought to keep up with Mel's long strides.

"Did you look inside?" Harper asked, the cold air causing her lungs to hurt. "Did you look in the trunk to make sure Zoe isn't there? If she was there all night, she could be frozen."

"Let's not get ahead of ourselves," Mel chided. "All we have is a car so far."

They remained silent until they arrived at the vehicle in question. Immediately, Mel and Jared split, with each taking a different side of the vehicle.

"It looks clean," Mel noted, shielding his eyes from the limited sun. "Zoe definitely isn't in there."

"No, but her hat is," Jared said, pointing toward a spot behind the passenger seat. "She was wearing a hat with cat ears, right?"

Harper nodded, her stomach twisting as she looked over his shoulder. "That's too small to be an adult's hat."

"We need to open the trunk right now," Jared insisted, tugging on the passenger side door. "It's locked."

Mel tried his side, but it didn't open. "Stand back," he ordered David, using the butt of his gun and smashing it against the window. The glass shattered into a million pieces, and Mel reached inside and hit the trunk button on the dash. "Go," he ordered Jared, inclining his chin.

Jared didn't need to be told twice. He raced to the back of the car and grabbed the trunk lid, internally praying he wasn't about to see the worst thing in the world, and then shoved it open. To his immense relief, the trunk was empty. There was no little girl trapped inside.

"Phew," he muttered under his breath, wiping his brow with the back of his hand. It was a true testament to his fear that he managed to work up a sweat in below-freezing temperatures.

"She's not in there," Harper said, relief positively rolling off her. "That's good, right?"

"It's better than the alternative," Mel said. "We still have a problem, though. If Jessica had Zoe's hat, where is she?"

"I don't know, but this case is getting weirder and weirder," Jared said. "None of this makes any sense."

"Which is why we have to start at the beginning. I have no idea what's going on here, but we're missing something ... and it's something important."

Eleven

Jared took Harper to Jessica's house, but only because he hoped she would be able to find their missing ghost. He ordered her to stay in the car long enough to force open the front door — he was legitimately worried there would be a body inside — but when he came up empty, he briefly allowed her to enter.

"Don't touch anything, Heart," he warned, keeping watch out the front window. "You don't have much time. The state police are sending over a crime scene unit, and they should be here in ten minutes. No offense, but I don't want to explain what you're doing here. It didn't exactly go over well with the medical examiner."

Harper couldn't muster the energy to be offended. She didn't have time. Instead, she cruised through the house — keeping her mittens in place — and tried to swallow the bubble of disappointment clogging her throat by the time she was finished.

"She's not here."

"That's not unheard of, right?" Jared didn't want her feeling down, so he carefully ordered her hair and smiled. "You're the one who told me that new ghosts can't always control their environment so sometimes they come and go at odd intervals."

"I love it when you spout my ghost knowledge back to me," she said drily, shaking her head. "You're right, though. We can't force her to show up."

"Then there's nothing you can do." Jared flicked his eyes to the window to make sure the coast was still clear. "I called Zander. He's on his way. He says he'll keep you busy for the rest of the afternoon."

"That's a frightening thought," Mel muttered, joining them. "The last time he promised to keep me busy, he made me go to this freaky store in the mall where they sold pink suits. He insisted I try one on."

Jared tried to picture his partner in a pink suit. "That sounds like a pleasant afternoon. Please tell me there's video ... or at least a photograph."

"I threatened him with death if he tried," Mel said, slowly moving his eyes to Harper. "I don't want to kick you out, kid, but I don't think you should be here when the state police show up. You're going to be hard to explain."

Harper realized that without the gentle nudge. "I'll wait outside. Zander is on his way, right?"

Jared nodded. "You can sit in the cruiser if you want. It's warmer there. That we can explain by saying we were having lunch when the car was discovered. It's just ... ." He felt slimy suggesting that the state police would give them grief for bringing a ghost hunter to a potential crime scene, so he left the sentence hanging.

"I get it. You don't have to worry." She rolled up to the balls of her feet and pressed a kiss to the corner of his mouth. "Zander and I have shopping ahead of us. I still have a few last-minute items I want to get. I promised him a mall trip. Now seems as good a time as any since we can't do anything else."

"And you'll be safe at the mall." Jared smacked a loud kiss against her mouth when she moved to pull away. "I'll call you when I know more. The fact that Zoe isn't here is a good thing."

"No, actually, if Zoe was here and okay, that would be the best outcome available," Harper corrected, refusing to let him gloss over the situation. "The fact that she's not dead in this house somewhere — or in Jessica's vehicle — is only good because the alternative is unbearable."

"I can see you're not in the best frame of mind right now. I don't blame you. At least we have somewhere new to look."

"I hope you find something helpful."

"You and me both."

ONCE HARPER WAS removed from the situation — Jared stood at the window and made sure she was safely transferred to Zander's custody — the two police detectives broke apart and started searching the house. They were looking for any indication that Zoe had been present, however minuscule.

The state police crime team arrived shortly after Harper disappeared and immediately set out gathering fibers for later tests. The house itself wasn't overly clean, but it was far from dirty. Everything seemed to have a logical place, and Jessica couldn't be described as a hoarder.

"Anything?" Jared asked, walking into the home office and finding Mel on the floor going through files. "Please tell me she had a secret diary that laid out all her plans."

"I haven't found a diary." Mel's eyes never left the contents of the file he was perusing. "I did find this, though. It seems Jessica hired a private investigator two days ago."

Jared perked up almost instantly. "Are you serious?"

"I am indeed serious."

"Anyone we know?"

"I don't think you know him. I know him, though. Chet Masters. His office is in Mount Clemens."

"Does it say what he's required to do for her?"

"No, which I find suspicious." Mel rolled his neck and pursed his lips. "Have you found anything?"

"I did find one thing of interest." Jared motioned for Mel to follow him through the house, not stopping until he reached the back door. He pushed it open and pointed at the locking mechanism. "What does that look like to you?"

Mel leaned over so he could have a clear view. "It looks like someone tried to jimmy the lock."

"According to our friendly state police technicians, these are fresh grooves. They can tell because we haven't had a big storm in the past few days, and if we did, the wood would be more weathered."

"So ... someone broke into the house recently."

"Pretty much," Jared confirmed. "Now, in theory, it's possible that Jessica accidentally locked herself out of the house and had to break in herself."

"Why does your smug smile tell me you've already disproven that theory?"

Jared's smirk widened. "Because I checked under the flowerpot out here — I mean — who leaves a flower pot on the back porch through winter? — and there's a spare key underneath it. Jessica wouldn't need to jimmy her own lock."

"Someone else broke in."

"That's my guess."

"Maybe that's why she wanted Chet Masters. Perhaps he was going to beef up security for her."

"I think we need to pay him a visit to find out exactly what he was doing for her," Jared said. "Jessica didn't whack herself in the head with a rock. That's pretty obvious. And yet Zoe's hat was found in her car. We've yet to find anything else that suggests Zoe was ever in close proximity with Jessica."

"Someone was trying to frame Jessica, and killed her to do it," Mel mused. "I don't understand how killing her with a rock furthers that agenda, though. The killer had to know that was suspicious."

"Maybe things got out of hand."

"Maybe." Mel rolled his neck until it cracked, thoughtful. "I think we need to have a sit down with Chet."

"I'm all over that."

HARPER AND ZANDER VISITED their favorite shops in the mall, which only took thirty minutes because everything they used to love had closed down thanks to a shifting economy. Still, they went to the candle store so Zander could buy a perverted snowflake candle as a gag gift for Mel, and then stopped in a different store so Harper could pick out a pretty hat for Shawn.

Their next stop was the jewelry store, although neither of them were feeling in the mood to "ooh" and "aah" over trinkets when their minds kept wandering elsewhere.

"What did you get Jared?" Zander asked as he studied a diamond watch with muted interest.

"I was kind of thinking that he should be happy with the gift that is me," Harper replied, earning a snicker.

"That sounds like something I would say. I considered getting naked, putting a bow on myself, and letting Shawn unwrap me. It's weird, though, it was like he anticipated that. He said he expected a gift that didn't involve nudity. As if that's really a gift."

Harper chortled, genuinely amused. "Oh, you guys are so perfect for each other." She instinctively reached out and gave Zander's cheek a squeeze. "I can't tell you how happy I am that you guys found each other."

Zander's lips curved. "I did a pretty good job finding him, huh?"

"I think he did a pretty good job finding you."

"What about you and Jared? Which one of you found the other?"

"That's a good question." Harper moved around the edge of the jewelry case and leaned over to look at a watch. This one was less ornate than the one Zander picked out, which was to be expected. "Do you think Jared would like this?"

Zander shifted closer and followed her gaze. "It's nice. Kind of boring, if you ask me, but nice. Since Jared is often boring — especially when it comes to his personal style — that fits. Although, this is pretty expensive. Haven't you bought his big gift already?"

Harper opened her mouth to answer, her cheeks burning, but no sound came out.

"You haven't bought his big gift yet?" Zander's voice carried under normal circumstances, but now it was absolutely shrill. "Are you crazy?"

"I didn't know what to get him," Harper admitted, sheepish. "I've never really purchased a Christmas gift for a boyfriend before. I mean, technically I purchased something for Quinn, but we'd only been together for a short time and we were young so getting him a sweater and calling it a day was perfectly acceptable."

"Yes, well, you're a big girl now," Zander snapped. "How could you possibly think that not getting Jared a gift was okay?"

"I'm going to get him a gift." Harper's voice was unnaturally high. "I know I need to get him a gift. It's just ... what am I supposed to get him?"

"Why are you asking me?" Zander was furious. "I don't know what to get him. I barely know what to get my own boyfriend. You can't put your problems on me. Solve your own problems."

"But ... I don't know what to get him." Harper's eyes brimmed with tears. "What if I get something too small and make him feel unloved? What if I get something too big and hurt his feelings because he didn't spend as much on me? What if I buy eight things and he buys seven? It's just too much pressure."

"Oh, good grief." Zander rolled his eyes. "You're going to drive yourself insane if you keep this up. More importantly, you're going to drive me insane. Go big. Trust me. You'll never be able to top what he got you."

Zander realized he made a mistake the second the words were out of his mouth. It was too late to take them back.

Harper's eyes widened to the size of saucers as she rounded on Zander. "You know what he got me."

"No, I didn't say that."

"You do. You just said that I couldn't top his gift. That means you know what he got me." She grabbed his shirt, not caring in the least how he felt about wrinkles. "Tell me what I'm getting. Now! Tell me and then I can get him something appropriate."

Harper was the best friend Zander ever had. She was the yin to his yang, the cream to his coffee, the vinegar to his potato chips. No matter how much he loved her, however, he wouldn't ruin Jared's surprise.

"No." Zander calmly removed Harper's fingers from his shirt. "I made a promise, and I intend to keep it. The only thing I can tell you is that you're going to love it."

Desperation thick as a concrete wall washed over Harper. "What am I supposed to do if you won't tell me?"

"Follow your heart," Zander instructed. "It won't let you down."

Harper wasn't sure that was true. "It allowed me to keep dating Quinn even though I knew he was a tool."

"You were close to breaking that off. You just don't remember it because things changed when he went missing. Don't dwell on that. You're an adult now. You know how to give Jared exactly what he needs. Don't forget that."

Harper scowled. "We're going to fight about this like you wouldn't believe when we don't have an audience."

"I'm looking forward to it."

CHET, TWO DAYS' WORTH of stubble on his cheeks, drank straight from a bottle of Maalox as he rested his feet on his desk and regarded Jared and Mel with a dubious look.

"To what do I owe the pleasure, gentlemen?" he drawled lazily.

"We need to talk to you about Jessica Hayden," Mel replied without hesitation.

Chet narrowed his eyes. "Who is that?"

"Don't play games," Mel chided. "We don't have time for it."

"We know she was your client," Jared added.

"Well, since you already know that, you should probably also know that I can't talk about my clients because it's a breach of trust."

"She's dead," Mel declared.

Whatever he was expecting, that wasn't it. Chet lowered his feet to the ground and leaned forward, suddenly keen. "Are you serious?"

"No, we make it a point of lying about people being dead right before the holidays," Jared drawled. "It's how we get our kicks."

Chet slid him an annoyed look. "You're the new detective around Whisper Cove, right? The one dating the ghost hunter."

The statement caught Jared off guard. "What makes you say that?"

"I've seen you on the news recently, and in my job, it pays to watch the news. Your girlfriend was the one almost killed in the field. I saw you two on camera together in a few of the shots. She's pretty."

"She's not up for discussion," Jared shot back. "We're here to talk about Jessica, who was bashed in the head sometime yesterday afternoon and left in a park."

"A park?" Chet furrowed his brow. "That's weird, right?"

"What's even weirder is that we were trying to track her down because we had some questions to ask her about the disappearance of Zoe Mathers," Mel volunteered. "We need to know that she had no part in the kidnapping. If she did, we need to know who her partner was, because it seems to me, the partner is off the rails."

"And you just assume I have knowledge of this?" Chet was incredulous. "Why would I possibly want to participate in the kidnapping of a child?"

"I don't know. We need to know why Jessica hired you, though."

"How did you even know about our arrangement?"

"She had a file in her office."

"Ugh." Chet slapped his hand to his forehead. "I knew she was going to be a pain. Everyone knows you don't leave a file laying around."

"Perhaps she didn't know she was going to die," Jared suggested. "Speaking of that, if you know anything about this, now would be a good time to tell us."

"I don't know anything about this particular situation," Chet replied, exhaling heavily. "Trust me. If I knew she was going to die, I would've stopped it. I liked her. She wasn't a pain."

"Why did she come to you?"

"Because she wanted me to follow her ex-boyfriend," Chet answered, causing Jared to wrinkle his forehead. "She was convinced he was cheating on her with another woman and she wanted proof."

"Why, though?" Mel queried. "They weren't married. It's not as if she could get extra money from him in a divorce if she proved infidelity. How would she benefit?"

"I brought up the same concerns. She didn't care. She wanted to catch him cheating. I suggested that perhaps her ego couldn't take being dumped for no reason and she had to blame someone else, but she didn't agree with me."

"I don't suppose she gave you an idea of who he was supposedly cheating with, did she?" Jared asked, his mind busy. "Her mother never mentioned her suspicions about infidelity. Perhaps that was something Jessica came up with after that fact."

"I guess that's possible, but she had a list of things that she found 'funny.'" Chet held up his hands and made the appropriate air quotes. "She was a bit manic when she stopped in, gave me the impression that she'd been up all night making this list."

"When was this?"

Chet checked his file and read back the date, allowing Jared to do the math in his head.

"That would've been the day after Luke broke up with her," he mused. "He said she took it relatively well, but it sounds like she was just saving face."

"Where did she want you to follow Luke?" Mel asked. "I mean ... where did she think he was meeting this girlfriend?"

"She didn't give me a specific place. She just wanted me to follow him after work every night for a week. She paid in advance."

"Did you follow him?"

Chet nodded. "Three nights in a row, although I backed off when word started spreading about the kid going missing. I knew through my own research that he was the father and I didn't want to get caught sitting outside his house."

"Yes, you're a real paragon of virtue," Jared drawled. "Did Luke go anywhere the nights you were watching him?"

"No. As a matter of fact, he went straight home and stayed in the house. I looked through a window twice, convinced he must be looking at porn on the internet or something. He wasn't, though. He was watching Netflix and drinking beer."

Jared and Mel exchanged a quick look.

"Who was Jessica convinced he was having an affair with?" Mel asked finally.

"The ex. Ally Bishop."

"Oh, geez." Jared pressed the heel of his hand to his forehead. "We just made a really big circle."

Mel bobbed his head. "Yup, and I don't like where this is headed. Not one little bit."

Twelve

Harper bought the watch ... and a few other things. She didn't leave the mall until her arms felt tired thanks to carrying heavy bags. Each time she purchased an item, she looked to Zander to see if it would be enough. To his credit, he managed to keep a straight face ... but just barely.

When they returned home, Harper decided to carry Jared's packages to the new house so she could wrap them in peace. Zander was fine with that, he had his own wrapping to do, and once left to her own devices Harper was able to allow her mind to drift as she wrapped.

She thought it would be panic about Jared's Christmas gift that took over her mind — and she was right to some extent — but it was more than that. Thoughts of Jared led to thoughts of Luke and Ally. At some point, Ally must have convinced herself that things would work with Luke. Even after he melted down about the pregnancy, all signs pointed to the fact that she thought he would get over himself.

He never did ... and that had to hurt.

It took Harper about an hour to wrap everything, and when she was done, she placed the items in a box in the front closet and tugged on her coat. She had an idea that had been forming, and she couldn't shove it out of her head.

With that in mind, she left a note for Jared on the counter and then pointed herself toward Luke's house. She had two reasons for heading in that direction. The first was Jessica. If she was really as obsessed with Luke as some people seemed to indicate, there was every chance her ghost was hanging around his house so she could watch him. If she wasn't there, though, it wouldn't be a total loss. She had a few things to say to Luke, and she didn't think she could keep them in much longer.

Harper parked in front of the house, taking a long moment to scan each side for hints of ghostly movement. There was nothing, and she couldn't help feeling disappointed as she exited her car.

It never occurred to her that Jared might be furious when he found out about her activities. Sure, in the back of her head she acknowledged that he was overprotective and prone to fits of exaggerated bossiness, but she legitimately didn't think she was doing anything wrong.

The feeling waned a bit when Luke answered the door wearing nothing but a loose robe and a pair of boxer shorts. He smelled like stale beer … and lack of a shower, and his eyes were bleary when he focused on Harper.

"You're the ghost chick."

Harper merely shrugged at the greeting. She'd been called worse things. "I'm Harper Harlow." She extended her hand. "We've actually met several times throughout the years, but you probably don't remember that."

Luke slowly accepted her hand and looked her up and down, causing Harper to uncomfortably shift from one foot to the other thanks to the nature of his gaze. Finally, she did something that she found irritating in other people, but she couldn't help herself. She decided to shut Luke down with a proactive strike.

"I'm living with Jared Monroe, who happens to be a detective on the Whisper Cove Police Department," she offered. "You might not want to stare too long."

Abashed at being caught, Luke quickly released her hand and rubbed his cheeks to wake up. "I'm sorry. I was just thinking about some things I've heard about you." He didn't ask why she was there, instead turning on his heel and heading inside the house. Harper took that as an invitation since he didn't slam the door in her face. "You can talk to ghosts. It says that right on your office window."

"I can," Harper agreed. Now was not the time to pussyfoot around Luke's personal prejudices. If he didn't like her, she didn't really care. "I've been able to see ghosts since I was a kid."

Luke paused by the stove as he reached for the teakettle. "Have you seen Zoe?" He almost looked fearful to hear the answer.

Harper shook her head. "No. I don't want to see her, and so far I haven't. I have seen Jessica, though."

"You've seen Jessica where?"

"She was at the candlelight vigil last night," Harper replied absently, something occurring to her after the fact. "You weren't at the candlelight vigil."

Luke merely shrugged as he filled the teakettle and placed it on a burner. "I didn't think I would be welcome there. I didn't want to hurt Ally further by taking attention away from her. That didn't seem fair."

Harper cocked a challenging eyebrow. "Since when have you felt like being fair to her? It seems to me, you were unfair to her from the start."

"You would say that," Luke muttered, rubbing the back of his neck. "You don't understand how difficult it was for me. I really liked Ally. I mean ... *really* liked her. I thought there was a chance we might make it longer than my other relationships.

"I never thought we would make it all the way because the idea terrified me," he continued. "I thought maybe she could somehow break the curse I was mired in, though. I kind of wanted to be a better man when I was with her."

Even though he was opening himself up, Harper found she wanted to beat his head into a cupboard. "You're basically saying you don't take any personal responsibility for the things you've done."

Luke let loose a sigh. "That's not what I'm saying. It's just ... I liked playing the field. I liked jumping from girlfriend to girlfriend. I didn't like the idea of intimacy because it always seemed to backfire on me.

"If I remembered something wrong, they would blame me for not caring enough to remember," he continued. "If I forgot something outright, they would accuse me of being self-absorbed. I realized at some point that if they already thought I was self-absorbed, then it was best to honestly be self-absorbed because very little would be expected of me.

"That worked out well for a long time," he continued. "I had no problem breaking hearts ... until Ally."

Despite herself, Harper felt sorry for him because of the hangdog expression on his face. "You loved Ally, didn't you?"

Luke's face flushed dark red. "I ... no. I've never been in love with anyone."

Because he avoided eye contact, Harper knew he was lying. "Oh, geez. You loved Ally." She rolled her neck as she thought back four years before. "I remember people talking about you around then. I was kind of in a haze because I had my own issues, but I remember sitting at the coffee shop one day and you went walking by with Ally.

"People still had hope for you then," she continued, amused at the way he grimaced. "They thought you were one of those guys who was going to sow his wild oats for a few years and then settle down. They all claimed they'd seen it before and that you weren't really a bad guy."

"Oh, yeah?" Luke didn't look convinced. "Most people nowadays believe I'm the worst guy."

"That's because you did some really horrible things when Ally was pregnant. I mean ... accusing her of drugging you. What was up with that?"

Luke's mouth opened and closed, making him look like a guppy gasping for breath, and finally he merely shook his head.

"You don't know why you did that?" Harper challenged, refusing to let him off the hook. "That was such a specific accusation that I would think you'd never forget the reasoning behind it."

"Ugh. You're a real ball buster, aren't you?" Luke scowled. His hair was filthy— it had clearly been days since he showered — but his eyes flashed with true outrage for the first time since Harper entered the house. "I didn't want to be a father. It scared the crap out of me. Like ... seriously. My stomach was upset for weeks and I had digestive issues in the bathroom because of it."

Harper made a face. "That was a massive overshare." She was officially disgusted. "Why would you tell me that?"

Luke shrugged. "I just want someone to understand that I didn't set out to be the worst guy in town."

"Then why did you allow it to happen?" Harper challenged. "I can see being surprised. While I don't agree with it, I can see momentarily freaking out and saying something stupid. You abandoned your child, though. You accused her mother of heinous things."

"Do you think I'm not aware of that?" Luke was morose. "Do you think I don't know that I'm a complete and total tool?"

"And yet, knowing that, you still haven't made things right with your child." Harper's voice was soft. "Why haven't you even met Zoe? She's adorable, by the way. She's precocious and she knows weird things.

"Like, right around Halloween, Zander and I were in the coffee shop and Ally was there with Zoe," she continued. "Rose gave her a cake pop and Zoe had hot chocolate smeared around her mouth, but she lit up when she saw us.

"She heard things around town, you see," she said. "She heard that we were having a ghost tour and she wanted to go with us. She wanted to catch a ghost and put it on a leash so she would always have someone to clean her bedroom. She was adamant about it and no matter how we tried to explain about ghosts, she wouldn't back down.

"She's a stubborn ... and smart ... and really sweet little girl," she said. "We heard her telling Ally when we left that she really wanted the ghost for her mommy so she didn't always have to work so hard."

Luke made a strangled sound in the back of his throat. "She said that, huh?"

Harper didn't miss the fact that his eyes were glittery as she nodded. "She did say that. She loves her mother. I think she would love you, too, if you would simply get your head out of your behind."

Luke rubbed his forehead, lost. "I thought I would have more time."

"More time for what?"

"More time to get to know her, be her father."

"Well ... you still might. That doesn't change the fact that your child is missing and you seem to be hiding instead of looking for her. Have you left the house since you got the news? Have you taken a night off from drinking? Have you considered going to Ally and offering support?"

Luke balked. "I can't do that. She hates me. Now is not the time she'll want to see me."

"You might be surprised."

"I just ... it hurts to think about her," Luke admitted. "I've seen her around town. I watch when I think no one is looking. In the summer, they had that petting zoo thing and one of the local farmers had puppies. Zoe was there with Ally and she was begging for one of the puppies, but Ally told her no because she worked too much and it wouldn't be fair to the puppy.

"I wanted to step in right then, tell Zoe she could have that puppy and I would make sure it was taken care of," he continued. "I didn't, though. I hid in the shadows like a coward."

"If you want to be a father, why not approach Ally and tell her you've had a change of heart? She's a good person. She wouldn't cut you out of Ally's life for no good reason."

"Look around." Luke gestured at the mess of a kitchen. "Do I look like I would be a good father? There are beer cans everywhere ... and I haven't eaten anything other than pizza in a week."

"Those are things that can be fixed." Harper's voice was gentle. "You should probably cut down on the drinking regardless, but kids love pizza. You can still turn your life around and turn into a functioning member of society. You can still be a father."

"Not if she isn't found."

"Yeah, well ... ." Harper broke off when the doorbell rang. "Are you expecting someone?"

"No. I'll be right back."

Harper busied herself with the teakettle while he was gone, pouring two mugs of tea and sliding some of the beer bottles into cardboard sleeves to get them out of the way. She turned at the sound of feet and lowered voices, and when her gaze locked with Jared's furious brown orbs, she made a face.

"What are you doing here?" They asked each other at the same time.

"I asked you first," Jared snapped.

"You did not. We asked at the exact same time."

"No, I distinctly heard myself asking first."

"Oh, geez."

Mel coughed into his hand to draw their attention, his disgust at the ridiculous argument evident. "Let's focus on the important things, shall we? We need to ask you a few more questions, Luke."

"I figured when I saw you at the door." Luke joined Harper behind the counter and grabbed a garbage bag from underneath the sink so they could start loading pizza boxes into it. "Fire away. I'm taking it you have no leads so you have to keep circling around to me or be sure."

Jared cocked an eyebrow in Harper's direction. "Didn't you tell him where we were?"

She shook her head. "I was here to talk about something else."

"What?"

"The fact that I'm a crappy father and it's not too late to turn things around if we ever get Zoe back," Luke replied for her. "Sadly, I still want to smack myself for being such a fool."

"I think you'll have to get in line because half the town feels that way," Mel said. "We have serious questions, though, and they might come as a bit of a surprise so maybe you should sit down."

Instead of acquiescing, Luke merely shook his head. "I've been sitting down and feeling sorry for myself for days. Why don't you just tell me why you're here, and if I need to sit down, I will. How does that sound?"

"It's up to you." Mel tugged on his shirt to straighten it. "You obviously know about Jessica's death," he started.

"What?" Luke whipped his head toward the two police detectives. "Jessica is dead?"

"You didn't tell him?" Jared asked Harper, his confusion returning.

"Well, I mentioned seeing Jessica dead," Harper said. "He didn't say anything so I assumed he knew."

"I didn't realize that's what you were saying," Luke barked, his eyes flashing. "I didn't understand what you meant when you said you saw her. I ... how did she die?"

Jared and Mel exchanged a quick look.

"She was bashed over the head with a rock in the park," Jared replied after a beat. "It happened sometime yesterday, although the medical examiner is still working on a firm time of death."

"But ... why?"

"We don't know, but we believe it has to do with Zoe," Jared replied honestly. "We found her hat in the backseat of Jessica's car."

"What?" Luke's expression was wild as he looked to Harper for confirmation. "I don't understand," he said when she nodded. "Why would Jessica take Zoe? That makes no sense."

"Jessica seemed to be having a bit of trouble with your breakup," Jared explained. "She was ... struggling."

"But she was no worse than the others when I told her," Luke argued. "Sure, she called me names and said I was less than a man, but that's par for the course and I'm used to it. She didn't act like she was out of control or anything."

"Well, apparently she was good at hiding it," Mel said. "She hired a private investigator to follow you. His name is Chet Masters. We found financial records and had a meeting with him about an hour ago. He confirmed that she was obsessed with you and wanted to know what you were up to."

"This is unbelievable." Luke dropped the garbage bag and slowly sank to the linoleum floor, his back to the cupboards. "I don't understand this. Are you saying you believe Jessica had something to do with Zoe's disappearance? If so, where is she now? Zoe, I mean. I'm assuming Jessica is in the morgue."

"There are a couple of possibilities." Mel chose his words carefully. "One is that Jessica took Zoe as payback and killed her in a fit of rage, perhaps leaving her body out in the woods somewhere. We might never find her if that's the case."

"I don't believe that's true," Harper argued. "I think Zoe is still alive."

Mel ignored her and remained focused on Luke. "The other possibility is that Jessica was working with someone, perhaps holding on to

Zoe in an attempt to create panic. She might've planned to say she stumbled across Zoe, return her, and bask in the limelight of being a hero. Surely you couldn't ignore her if she did that."

"That seems a little far out there," Luke hedged. "I mean … she hired a private investigator to watch me. That must have been quite the boring job over the last few days."

"That's exactly what Chet said," Mel confirmed. "Apparently Jessica had it in her head that you broke up with her for another woman."

"I'm not seeing anyone right now. I don't foresee that changing anytime soon, especially with Zoe being missing."

"Yes, well, Jessica was convinced you were seeing Ally."

Luke's mouth dropped open. "What?"

"Yes. She said she was convinced you were going back to Ally and she wanted proof of it to confront you with. Do you have any idea why she would believe that?"

"No. Unless … well, I might have mentioned to her once that I made a mistake with Ally. I've been thinking about that a lot lately. I wasn't just talking about the relationship, though. I was talking about Zoe."

"Which might have been enough to set Jessica off," Jared mused.

"So … this is my fault?" Luke looked horrified at the prospect. "Am I the reason that Ally might lose Zoe forever?"

"We don't know," Mel replied simply. "As for never seeing her again, we don't know that's the case. There's still hope."

"What hope?" Luke was miserable as he buried his face in his hands. "What have I done? I can't believe this is my fault."

Harper wanted to offer him comfort, but she didn't know how to give it. It was looking more and more likely that he was at the center of this. What that meant for Zoe, though, was anyone's guess.

Thirteen

Jared walked Harper out to her car when they were done interrogating Luke. He had a few questions for her, too, and she knew she wasn't going to like them.

"How was your day shopping with Zander?" he started.

Harper shrugged, noncommittal. "Not as much fun as I would've liked," she said truthfully. "He won't tell me what you got me, so I had to buy ten extra things to make sure I purchased you enough gifts."

Jared knit his eyebrows. "I think you're missing the meaning of Christmas."

"Perhaps," she admitted. "That's easy for you to say when you've apparently bought the perfect gift. I don't suppose you'll tell me what it is, will you?"

"No." Jared's lips curved as he shook his head. "You can wait until Christmas. As for the gifts ... I think you're the best gift I've ever received. I don't need anything else."

"Oh, so sweet." She tapped his chin. "That's what I told Zander and he said I was severely mistaken. Then he let slip that I would never be able to match your gift, and when I tried to browbeat him into telling me what it was, he refused to give me anything. I was a little disappointed."

Jared chuckled. "Leave it be. You'll be happy with the surprise when it comes."

"I guess." She flicked her eyes to her car, and the light dusting of snow covering it. "We're supposed to get a few inches tonight. How long until you come home?"

"It's still going to be a few hours. We have to speak to Jessica's mother. She's been notified about her daughter's death, but we wanted to give her a bit of time to settle before going back. I'm not sure when I'll be home. Don't wait on dinner for me."

"I'll make sure you have something to eat when you get home." She breezily brushed a kiss against the corner of his mouth. "I'll see you later, huh?"

Jared knew exactly what she was doing and found it amusing … almost. There was no way he was going to let her slide, though, so he grabbed her wrist before she could ease away. "Heart, we're not done here."

Harper briefly pressed her eyes shut before planting a huge fake smile on her face. "Do you want to kiss me some more? I think I can make time."

"You're very cute. Like … so cute I just want to kiss you senseless." He tapped the end of her nose. "I'm not falling for this, though, and you know it. Why were you here? Oh, and Heart, don't leave anything out."

Harper let loose an exaggerated sigh. "I couldn't let things go, even after an afternoon of shopping with Zander. The part that bothered me the most was Luke, and since I was fairly certain you'd cleared him as a suspect, I decided there was no harm in stopping for a visit."

"I never said we'd cleared him as a suspect."

"So … you do suspect him?"

"I didn't say that either."

Harper frowned. "Jared, I wanted to talk to him about his choices. I think he gets it. He understands that leaving Ally while she was pregnant was probably the worst mistake of his life. Now, though, he's terrified that he's not going to be able to make up for it. I simply wanted to feel him out."

"And now that you have, are you going to stay out of it?"

"Of course not."

Jared sighed. "I knew you were going to say that."

"You know me well." She lightly patted his cheek and grinned. "I can't let it go. You know that as well as me. If you try to force the matter, we're going to fight. Do you want to fight at Christmas?"

"Oh, that was low." He made a tsking sound in the back of his throat as he shook his head. "That was really low."

"It's the truth. I can't look away. Zoe is out there. I feel it here." She tapped the spot above her heart.

Jared grabbed her hand and moved it to the spot over his heart. "Do you have any idea of what I feel here when I look at you?"

She nodded, solemn. "Probably the same thing I feel."

"I'm a competitive soul so I like to think I feel it just a little bit more than you." His grin was lightning quick. "I need you to stay safe. I don't want you running around and finding trouble. Just ... promise me you'll be careful."

"I promise. I'll also have something warm ready for your dinner when you get home."

"Then we can properly make up after I eat," he teased.

"I didn't think this was much of a fight. Do we need to make up?"

He shrugged. "I happen to like making up. If we have to fake another fight to do it, we'll merely have to suck it up."

She returned his smile. "Maybe you'll let what I'm getting for Christmas slip during the fight."

"Not a chance."

EVEN THOUGH SHAWN AND Zander were annoyed when Harper announced they were going back to the park, they bundled up in five different layers and insisted on accompanying her. Since it was Michigan in December, that meant it got dark before six o'clock. While Harper might not have been an obvious target, there was no way they intended to simply let her wander around after dark without chaperones.

"I don't understand why we're coming back to the park," Shawn admitted as Zander killed the engine to his truck and hopped out.

They were parked on the road located on the far side of the park so as not to draw attention to themselves, and it was so cold their breath came out in foggy batches as their feet crunched against the snow softly landing on the ground.

"We're looking for Jessica," Harper replied, her eyes keen as she scanned the darkness. "Zander, did you bring the flashlights I asked for?"

He made a growling sound before turning around to tug open the truck door. He rummaged behind the seat for what felt like a really long time before returning with three flashlights which he proceeded to dole out. "Happy?"

"You're in a mood," Harper muttered, making a face. "No one made you come. I was perfectly willing to make the trek by myself."

"Yes, and can you imagine the meltdown we would've been facing when Jared got home and realized we'd allowed you to wander around in the woods by yourself with a killer on the loose? Like I really have the energy to put up with that."

"This is hardly the woods," she scoffed, flicking on her flashlight and pointing it toward the trees. "No one would dare come after me here. We're close to the middle of town."

"Not really," Shawn argued, pointing his beam in the direction of downtown. "That's quite a walk ... and it's so dark, no one would be able to see you unless they were looking directly at you. When you add in the fact that it's cold enough to force everyone inside, it wouldn't have been wise to come out here alone."

"Well, I'm thankful you came with me." Harper smiled at him. "You're a prince amongst men."

"Hey!" Zander barreled between them, his eyes on fire. "I'm a prince amongst me. Me!" He thumped his chest to make sure all eyes were on him. "In fact, I'm better than a prince. I'm a king amongst men. You guys are simply my court jester and lady-in-waiting."

"Wait ... ." Shawn drew his eyebrows together. "Am I the jester or lady-in-waiting?"

Harper giggled as she shifted her flashlight to a clump of bushes about twenty feet away. "I don't want to be the jester, so that has to be you. In fact ... ." She trailed off when the beam bounced over a ghostly face. Slowly, she tracked the light back to the spot where she saw a pair of dead eyes staring at her and sucked in a breath when she recognized Jessica. The woman looked almost blue in the lighting, and it was an eerie sight.

"She's here," Harper said quietly, exhaling heavily.

"Well, that's good," Zander said, putting his hand to her back. "Get this conversation started so we can get out of here. It's freaky cold and I want to build a fire when we get back to the house."

"That's the plan." Harper forced a smile that felt somehow unnatural and took a tentative step forward. "Jessica, do you know where you are?"

The woman merely stared.

"Do you know what happened to you?" Harper asked, unsure how far she should press the obviously traumatized woman. "We want to help."

"We definitely want to help," Zander agreed. "It would be easier if you would join us in my truck, though. I invite you in for a conversation ... not to haunt it or anything. We're still alive so we shouldn't have to suffer to get information."

Shawn slid his boyfriend a sidelong look. "I thought the invitation thing was only an issue if you were dealing with vampires."

Zander's glare was withering. "It could be true for more than one thing. I'm simply covering my bases."

"Oh, well, good." Shawn shook his head. "I would hate to have to deal with ghosts who refuse to leave after the fact."

"Shut up," Harper barked, never moving her eyes from Jessica's sad face. "Jessica, we need your help. There's a little girl who is still out there, missing. Are you aware of what happened to Zoe Mathers?"

For the first time since Harper started talking, Jessica's expression changed and she registered something the woman said. "Zoe," she murmured, shaking her head. "I ... think I knew she was missing. There was a candlelight vigil the other night. I attended it. That's the last thing I remember."

Harper tilted her head to the side, conflicted. "You were already dead at the time of the candlelight vigil," she corrected finally. Ghosts often had screwed-up inner clocks, but no good could come of letting the ghost drift without actual knowledge. "You died before then. I believe it was earlier in the day."

"I wasn't at the vigil?" She screwed her face up in concentration. "That doesn't sound right. I remember being there."

"You were. I saw you there. It's just ... you were already a ghost."

"Is that what I am?" Jessica looked intrigued despite herself. "I didn't know I was a ghost." She studied her hand, as if seeing it for the first time. "How did I become a ghost?"

"That's what we're here to ask you," Harper replied simply. "We want to know what happened to you. We believe you were struck from behind here, right in this park."

"Struck from behind." Jessica repeated the words. She seemed ridiculously slow, and Harper was starting to wonder if that was a byproduct of the weather. Maybe a new ghost had issues when it was cold. That was something she hadn't considered before, but she could hardly rule it out now. "Maybe. I don't know. Everything is jumbled."

"Okay." Harper decided to take a different approach. "What can you tell me about Luke Mathers?"

"What?" This time there was definite life in Jessica's eyes as she snapped her head in Harper's direction. "Is Luke here? Has he come to see me?"

Harper felt sad for the woman. She was a little pathetic, after all, and completely lost. That was not something Harper could focus on given the current circumstances, though. "Luke is at home dealing with things. With Zoe missing, he's had to answer a lot of questions."

"So ... he's not here?"

"No. He's not here. He's at home, although he knows you hired a private investigator to spy on him."

Jessica's face crumbled as she started making odd sobbing noises that set Harper's teeth on edge. "He knows about that? Oh, how embarrassing."

"Yes, that's what's important now," Harper deadpanned. "We should worry about how embarrassed you are. Hey! Look at me!" She snapped her fingers to get Jessica's attention. "I'm sorry for what happened to you. I really am. I hope you weren't involved in Zoe's kidnapping because it will make me regret feeling sorry for you, but right now I'm sympathetic.

"There's nothing we can do to help you but find your killer, though," she continued. "We can't do that until we find whoever kidnapped Zoe. I don't know a lot, but I know they're the same person. So, we need to know who killed you."

"I don't know who killed me." Jessica's voice was firm as she collected herself. Harper's words obviously had a stinging effect, because she stopped feeling sorry for herself and focused on the issues at hand. "I don't remember a lot."

"Why did you hire someone to follow Luke? Did you really think that would work to get him back?"

"I felt him pulling away," Jessica explained. "Weeks before he actually called it quits, I felt it. He admitted something to me one night, and I couldn't get it out of my mind. It bothered me a lot, but he never said anything similar again so I let it go."

"What did he say?" Harper asked, curious despite herself.

"We'd been drinking and were walking home from the bar. I said the worst mistake I ever made was dying my hair blue when I was in high school. It was wrong for my coloring and washed me out."

Harper had no idea where she was going with this. "Okay."

"He said that the worst thing he ever did was abandon Ally and Zoe," she continued. "He said that he would never be able to make up for it no matter how hard he tried. That's when I knew things would never be how I wanted them to be, although I fought it for a long time because I didn't want to admit defeat."

"So, you assumed he was going to go back to Ally, and that's why he broke up with you."

"He claimed it wasn't true, but I wanted proof."

"Did you take Zoe? Did you plot to take her?"

"No. I might be immature and full of myself, but I would never hurt a child."

Harper believed that. "Okay. We'll figure out who did this, Jessica. In the meantime, you might not want to hang around this place. I think it's slowing your reactions. Go home, to your house or your mother's place. Warm up. You might be able to think better after that."

"Sure. I guess it couldn't hurt."

JARED WAS EXHAUSTED WHEN HE walked into the kitchen shortly before nine and found Harper, Zander, and Shawn cleaning up after dinner.

"Hey." He moved immediately to Harper and gave her a long kiss, his fingers chilly from the cold outside. "How did things go for you tonight?"

"Pretty good," Harper replied. "I found Jessica's ghost. She doesn't know who killed her, but she swears up and down she didn't have anything to do with Zoe's kidnapping."

"Do you believe her?"

"I think I do."

"We have dinner warm for you in the oven," Shawn offered, pulling open the range door and retrieving a foil-covered plate. "Meatloaf, mashed potatoes, gravy, and green beans."

"Wow. Comfort food." Jared gladly accepted the plate and moved toward the table. "If Jessica had nothing to do with Zoe's kidnapping, that means someone wanted to point the finger at her."

"She makes an intriguing patsy," Shawn agreed. "She was obviously obsessed with Luke to the point where she was asking about him tonight, but from what Harper said, she was well aware that Luke had regrets about leaving Ally and knew she didn't stand a chance against the family he'd left behind when it finally came time for Luke to grow up."

"Yeah, it's a difficult situation," Jared agreed. "I need to think on it overnight. My head feels like mush."

"That's because you're working too hard." Harper sat next to him and moved her hand over his back. "Did you get anywhere tonight?"

"We talked to Jessica's mother. She was a mess and couldn't offer us much help. Everything else is a dead end. I can't help but think we're missing something."

"Yes, well ... ." Harper trailed off, pursing her lips. She had no idea what to offer to make him feel better.

Jared made a happy groaning sound as he dug into his food. "This is amazing. Zander, you outdid yourself."

"How do you know I didn't cook?" Harper asked suspiciously, annoyance evident when everyone in the room started laughing. "I don't think that's an outrageous question."

"You have many fine attributes, Heart, but cooking isn't one of them," Jared offered. "Oh, and by the way, I'm picking up my mother at the airport tomorrow morning, so I was hoping we could get together for lunch before I have to cut her loose and go back to the case."

Harper almost fell out of her chair she was so surprised. "What?"

"My mother," he repeated. "Did you forget she was coming?"

"I thought that was still up in the air."

Jared made a face. "Christmas is almost here. Why would it still be up in the air? I told you she was coming."

"Yes, but then I never heard another thing about it. I figured she changed her mind."

"Well, she didn't. She'll be here tomorrow."

Harper was flabbergasted. "Where is she going to stay?"

"The new house. That's why we bought the fancy guest sheets."

"But ... the room isn't ready."

"Well, I guess you'll have something to keep yourself out of trouble tomorrow morning, huh?"

Harper narrowed her eyes to glittery blue slits. "You planned this."

"Not at all. I'm going to take advantage of it, though. If you're entertaining my mother, you can't get into trouble."

"Don't underestimate her," Zander warned. "She can find trouble no matter the circumstances."

Harper was legitimately worried she was about to test that theory.

Fourteen

Harper couldn't help feeling that Jared somehow tricked her into believing his mother wasn't coming for Christmas. Sure, he told her months before that Pamela Monroe planned on visiting her son on the east side of the state over the holidays, but she pushed it out of her mind when no further conversation popped up.

Now she felt as if she was under the gun, and she wasn't happy about it.

"Get up," she ordered the next morning, skipping their usual snuggle fest and tugging at the duvet cover as he attempted to pull it over his head. "Get up. Get up. Get up!"

Jared merely opened one eye and stared at her. "It's not even seven yet, Heart. Why are you torturing me?"

"Why do you think?"

"Did you and Zander inadvertently swap bodies during the night?" Despite the early hour, Jared found he was enjoying the flustered appearance of his girlfriend. "Is this a *Freaky Friday* kind of a moment?"

"Do you think that's funny?"

"Not if I have to make out with Zander."

"Ha, ha, ha." She planted her hands on her hips. "Your mother is coming. You didn't tell me, and now we're way behind. We have to get over to the other house and put everything away before you leave to pick her up at the airport."

"Yeah, that's not going to happen." Jared refused to let her rile him. "Besides, you don't have to do anything at the other house. I told her it was going to be a mess."

"I have to get the guest room cleaned and find the bedding I bought ... and stash all the other boxes that are planted all over the house."

He smiled as she swiped at her hair, which only served to make it stand on end. She was absolutely adorable, and he could think of a few other things he wanted to do besides unpack boxes. "Come back to bed." He lifted the covers, slanting a pair of decidedly bedroom eyes in her direction. "I'll make it worth your while if you do."

On a normal morning, the invitation would've been impossible to deny. Harper was in a different world now. "Get up!"

"Geez, Heart, you're taking all the fun out of a lazy morning." He heaved out a sigh and rubbed his cheek. "Stop freaking out. She's not staying at the house. She doesn't care if the guest room is ready."

Harper stilled. "You said I had to get the guest room ready for her." Her tone was accusatory. "You said she was coming today."

"She *is* coming today. She's not staying at the house, though. I explained what a mess it is. She's staying in the hotel. I reserved her room weeks ago."

"But ... ."

"I was messing around with you last night," he volunteered. "I thought you would be more likely to stay at home rather than question potential kidnappers if you thought you had to clean the new house from top to bottom.

"However much I would like to keep you safe, though, I'm not comfortable lying," he continued. "I love you. Yada, yada, yada. She's staying at the hotel."

Harper relaxed, although only marginally. "Yada, yada, yada?"

His smile was back. "Come here and I'll show you what I mean by that."

She wagged a finger. "Uh-uh. You're in trouble. I can't believe you didn't at least tip me off that she was coming. I would've remembered if we set a date."

"She didn't give me much choice. I thought she forgot about it, too. She called three weeks ago to tell me, I was surprised at the time, and then I forgot."

"You forgot?"

"Hey, we've had a lot going on. Between your ex-boyfriend coming back from the dead and a missing girl, I've had other things on my mind. In truth, I thought I told you. It was only after you acted so shocked last night that I realized I hadn't."

"The house isn't ready for anyone to see it."

"Your parents have seen it."

"My parents are lost causes. Plus, they already like you. My mother thinks you're her only shot to unload me. She's embarrassed because she thinks I can't hold on to a man other than Zander."

"Your mother is much nicer to me than she is to you," he agreed. "You don't have to worry about my mother, though. She's easy. She never gives anyone a lick of trouble."

"Yeah, but ... what does she know about me?"

"That I love you."

"But ... what about the ghost stuff?"

Realization dawned on his face. "Oh, is that what you're worried about? She knows what you do for a living. I wouldn't keep that from her. Besides, you're proud of it. You should be, by the way. You're good at what you do. She'll probably ask a hundred questions, but she won't judge you for it."

"Yeah, but ... what if she doesn't like me?"

"Oh." He made a sad face to match hers. "Are you worried my mother won't like you? If so, don't. She's going to love you."

"Why?"

"Because you're lovable."

"I don't know." She glanced around, fearful. "I think I'm going to be sick. Maybe you should spend time with your mother and forget about me until after the holidays."

"No way." Jared turned serious. "I need you to be there with me for lunch. She's dying to meet you."

Harper sighed at his earnest expression. "Okay, but if she doesn't like me, I'm going to be all kinds of sad."

"You're not going to be sad." He held open his arms. "Come on. I want to show you how to yada, yada, yada."

No matter how much she wanted to fight the effort to smile, Harper found she didn't have the strength. "How can I turn down an offer like that?"

BECAUSE SHE WAS A BARREL OF nerves, Harper insisted Zander and Shawn go with her to lunch. Jared hadn't exactly okayed the guest list, but she was determined to have people there who genuinely liked her in case things went south.

They met at the hotel restaurant, and Harper was so jittery she bounced between Zander and Shawn as the hostess showed them to their table.

"How do I look?" she asked for the twentieth time.

"You look like I'm going to drown you in a toilet if you don't stop asking that question," Zander warned. "Seriously, I wouldn't let you leave the house looking like a fashion loser, would I?"

"No, but … ."

"Shut up." Zander was at the end of his rope as he smoothed his peach polo shirt. "You're driving me crazy. I'm sick of talking about your outfit. Let's talk about my outfit. How do I look?"

Shawn bit the inside of his cheek to keep from laughing. "You guys are quite the pair today."

"You should've seen us picking out stuff for prom," Zander said.

"I'm sure that was delightful."

"Then you're imagining it wrong," Harper said, making small animal noises in the back of her throat when she caught sight of Jared.

He sat at a round table in the center of the restaurant, three places set in addition to the ones he and his mother already occupied. The woman who sat with him was small — if Harper had to guess, she didn't clear five feet — and she was laughing so hard at something Jared told her that she didn't bother looking in their direction.

Jared, who was also laughing, did. He got to his feet when he saw her and extended his hand. "Hey, Mom, I have someone I want you to meet."

Pamela swiped at the corners of her eyes as she hurriedly climbed to a standing position. Her smile was so wide it threatened to swallow her entire face and she pushed Jared aside so she could get a better look at Harper.

"Oh, aren't you pretty? You are just adorable." Pamela threw her arms around Harper and engulfed her in a tight hug. Since Harper was a good seven inches taller than her, she had to bend over to accept the embrace. "She's lovely, Jared. Why didn't you tell me she's so pretty?"

"Yeah, Jared," Zander intoned, his tongue practically dripping with sarcasm. "Why did you tell your mother that Harper was such a dog?"

Jared's scowl was pronounced, but before he had a chance to give Zander a piece of his mind, Pamela was already directing her attention to Zander.

"You must be Zander. Jared said you were a flashy dresser. Look at this outfit. It reminds me of *Miami Vice*."

Harper tried to swallow her laughter, and couldn't. The mutinous look on Zander's face would have her laughing for days. "Oh, you're Sonny Crockett."

"Ha, ha, ha," Zander muttered, extending his hand. "Mrs. Monroe, I can't tell you how happy I am to meet you."

"Oh, that's not greeting enough for me." Pamela jerked Zander into an equally enthusiastic hug, laughing gaily as he awkwardly patted her back. "Jared was just telling me stories about you. I can't wait to hear more of them. It sounds as if you have quite the happy home."

"Not always," Jared muttered, earning a stern look from Harper as Pamela turned her attention to Shawn.

"That means you must be Shawn, right?" Her smile for him was as bright as for everybody else. "Jared says you're the peacemaker in the group when everyone starts fighting. It was the same way for me in my family because I had three sisters. I was always the peacemaker."

"It's not so bad," Shawn countered. "They only get out of hand four or five times a week."

"Oh, I can tell I'm going to like you." She gave him a hug, insisted that everyone call her "Pam," and had to be forced into her seat by

Jared before she would settle. "So, tell me everything about yourself." Her eyes were on Harper as she spoke. "I hear you can see ghosts. What's that like?"

"Oh, well … ." Harper paused, a menu in hand. "It's different. I don't know how to explain it."

"Basically she just stands around and talks to air most of the time," Zander explained. "Occasionally we get a rowdy ghost who doesn't want to leave and it throws things. While I can't see the ghosts, I can see the breaking crockery and stuff. That's always fun … unless I get hit in the head, which has been known to happen."

Harper made a face. "When have you ever found that fun?"

"Every single time."

"Yes, that's why you whine for hours after each event," she muttered, shaking her head. "Name one time you've ever liked it when a ghost threw something at you."

"I can't think of a time off hand, but I'm sure one exists." Zander raised a hand to quiet Harper so he could focus on Pam. "So, tell me about Jared as a kid. Was he a pain in the butt? Did he boss around the other kids? Did he always have freakishly large nipples?"

Harper was mortified by the last question. One look at Jared's ruddy cheeks told her he was equally flummoxed. Pam, though, laughed so hard Harper was surprised she didn't cough up a lung.

"Oh, you are everything Jared described," Pam enthused, rubbing her hands together. "He said you suck all the oxygen out of a room and he was right. I think we're going to be the best of friends."

Despite herself, Harper felt a small pang of jealousy lodge in her throat. Their whole lives, Zander was always the one who had an easier time making friends. She shouldn't have been surprised that he schmoozed Jared's mother before she had a chance to make an impression.

"That sounds delightful," Zander agreed. "I think you should bond with Harper, though. She has a terrible maternal influence. She needs more help than I do."

"Hey!" Harper shot him a look. "I have your mother."

Zander chuckled. "That's true. We've always shared my mother."

Pam's gaze was quizzical when it landed on Harper. "I was under the impression your parents were alive ... and local. Isn't that what you told me, Jared?"

"They're both local," Harper answered. "They're just ... a lot of work."

"So much work," Zander echoed. "This week they're fighting over garden gnomes."

"Fighting over?"

"They're getting divorced," Jared explained to his mother. "They've apparently been getting divorced for a long time. They fight over very odd things ... like spoons and garden gnomes."

"Perhaps they don't want to get divorced and the fights are merely a way to drag things out," Pam suggested.

"I've thought that myself, but they're hateful to each other," Harper admitted. "I love them both, but they're a lot of work. They're work together, and work apart. I don't know how things will finally end between them, but I try to stay out of the arguments. They're nothing but a headache."

"Of course they are." Pam turned solemn. "You seem sad, dear. Is something wrong? Are you upset that I came to town?"

"Oh, no," Harper said hurriedly, internally cursing herself. "It's just ... there's a lot going on right now and I let my mind drift for a second."

"To where?"

Harper pointed at the poster hanging on the wall on the far side of the restaurant. It was a missing person flier, and Zoe's face was front and center. "I was momentarily distracted by that."

Pam made a clucking sound with her tongue as she studied the poster. "Yes, Jared filled me in about the case on our drive back from the airport. That is simply tragic. Do you have any further leads?"

Jared shook his head. "No, but that's the reason I can't spend the afternoon with you. I need to check in with my partner. We're desperate to see if we can find a trace of that little girl so we can get her home in time for Christmas."

"Well, I think we all want that. Don't worry about me." She patted Jared's arm and focused on Harper. "If you're busy, that will give me time to get to know your girlfriend. I think we have a lot to discuss."

The way she said it made Harper nervous. "Oh, I'm not very interesting."

"You see and talk to ghosts."

"Yes, but that doesn't make me interesting."

"Don't listen to her, Pam," Zander chided, waving his hand. "She's extremely nervous, and when she's antsy like this, she says stupid things. She's the most fascinating person I know ... other than myself, I mean. I wouldn't have pledged myself as her non-romantic life mate if she wasn't interesting."

Pam's eyes lit with amusement. "She's nervous, huh? Why do you think that is?"

"I'm right here," Harper muttered, annoyed.

"I know you're here," Jared whispered, patting her knee under the table.

"You also knew I would bring Shawn and Zander. You had places already set for them."

"I knew you were afraid." His fingers were gentle as he tugged a strand of hair behind her ear. "There was no need for you to be afraid, but I knew you needed a safety blanket. That meant Zander."

"He's not my safety blanket."

"Oh, but he is." Jared gave her a soft kiss and smiled. "It's okay. Mom wants to meet everyone. I told her you were nervous."

"I have no idea why I'm so terrified," Harper admitted. "I've taken on hundreds of ghosts and never thought a thing of it. Meeting your mother, though, has completely knocked me for a loop."

"I already told you. She's going to love you no matter what." He gave her another kiss, this one so soft it nudged a sigh out of her.

She wasn't the only one at the table sighing, though. The moment their lips separated, Shawn and Pam both sighed, too. Zander merely glared at both of them and rolled his eyes.

"You guys are so cute I can't stand it," Pam said, shaking her head as her smile widened. "I mean ... look at you. You're so pretty together, and you're so romantic."

"They're schmaltzy," Zander corrected. "They're mushy freaks."

"Oh, you stop that." Pam wagged a finger at Zander. "They're adorable together. What's not to love?"

"I say the same thing to him at least once a week," Shawn volunteered. "He doesn't always agree with me."

"They're annoying," Zander complained. "They should spend less time worrying about each other and more time worrying about me. I'm the interesting one."

Pam's giggle was infectious as she stared at Zander. "You guys have quite the little family, don't you? I was worried about Jared moving to the other side of the state because we had no family over here. It looks like I didn't need to worry. He merely started a new one."

Jared's grin was indulgent. "I like most of my new family. However, if you want to take Zander with you to the other side of the state when you go, Mom, I would be fine with it."

"Ha, ha," Zander muttered as Pam clapped.

"Just delightful," she enthused. "I can't wait to spend the afternoon with all of you."

Harper wasn't sure she felt the same way, but the nerves from earlier were mostly gone. "We're looking forward to it, too. It's going to be a great afternoon."

Fifteen

Harper managed to loosen up over lunch, and by the end of the meal she was laughing and having a grand time. Pam was so amiable and easy — something she wasn't used to with her own parents — she found she liked the woman, immensely. That made bonding with her a joy rather than a chore.

Once lunch was finished, Jared had to excuse himself to head to the station. He promised to keep in touch and join the small group as soon as possible. That left Harper, Zander, and Shawn to give Pam a short tour of Whisper Cove (it could hardly be long because the town was so tiny) before heading over to the houses.

Pam loved the beach locale, gushed over Jason's restaurant and the view. She laughed at the kitschy shops and happily drank coffee from Rose's place before absolutely freaking (in a good way) over the new house. She ignored the boxes spread everywhere in the living room and kitchen, commented on the endless potential of the space, and chuckled when Harper pointed out the back window and showed her the spot where they were going to put a hammock.

By the time they returned to the other house, Zander was in a mood because it was time to start his holiday baking extravaganza. Harper worried Pam would be bored hanging around the house and was debating a trip to the mall when the older woman declared she absolutely loved baking and insisted on serving as Zander's apprentice. This was too much power for Zander, who roped in Harper and Shawn to help, too, so by the time Jared returned to the house early in the afternoon, the smell of baking cookies wafted through the house and the laughter in the kitchen was contagious.

"What are you doing home so early?" Harper asked as she approached him, wiping her hands on the apron Zander supplied.

"And hello to you, too," Jared drawled, amused. He swiped at a light dusting of flour on her face and grinned. "Have you been replaced by an android?"

Harper was confused. "What?"

"An android," he repeated. "I didn't know you could bake. I'm worried this is the opening scene of our own version of *Invasion of the Body Snatchers* or something."

Harper's lips curved down. "Ha, ha, ha. You're a funny guy."

"If I didn't become a cop, I would've become a clown," he agreed, wrapping his arms around her slim waist and giving her a kiss. "How are things going?" he whispered so only she could hear. "Are you okay?"

"Your mother is wonderful," Harper replied honestly. "She hasn't made one passive aggressive comment about my outfit."

Amused, Jared placed both hands on her cheeks and smacked a theatrical kiss against her lips. "My mother doesn't care about things like that."

"She loves Zander."

Jared slid his eyes to the kitchen, watching as Zander barked orders. Pam followed them without complaint while Shawn rolled his eyes. "She loves Zander because she knows that Zander is the key to your heart."

"I think that's a bit of an exaggeration."

"No, it's not." His smile was rueful. "I knew when we met that I was going to have to get on Zander's good side if I expected to have a chance with you. He's too important for you to disregard his opinion, so even though he drives you nuts, you listen to every word he says."

"Not *every* word." Harper was firm. "An hour ago he was explaining his theory of why all men should wear pink and I totally tuned him out."

Jared chuckled. "Fair enough."

"Hey, you two, stop smooching over there and get with the program," Zander ordered, drawing their attention. "Harper, you're supposed to be handling the sprinkles on the Christmas tree cookies. I don't see much sprinkling going on."

Jared turned to glare at Zander and found his mother staring at him with thoughtful eyes. "What are you smiling at, Mom?" he asked after a beat.

"You." Pam beamed. "You're very happy together. That's exactly what a mother wants to see."

"Harper definitely makes me happy," Jared agreed. "I could take or leave Zander, though."

"Do you know what makes me happy?" Zander challenged, ignoring the dig.

"I'm going to guess cookies," Shawn automatically answered.

"That would be it," Zander confirmed without hesitation.

Harper snorted and pressed another kiss to the corner of Jared's mouth before turning back. "I guess my presence is needed in the kitchen. The world will surely end if I don't sprinkle like I'm supposed to. I am curious what you're doing home so early, though. I thought you would be a few more hours."

"There's nothing I can do right now," Jared admitted. "I have files for sex offenders in the area and I'm going through them. The state police have dogs at Jessica's house trying to pick up Zoe's scent. Days after the fact, they probably won't pick up anything if she was only outside or in the driveway. If she was in the house, though, they should know."

"What will it mean if she was in the house?"

"I have no idea." Jared tugged a frustrated hand through his hair. "We don't know where to look. I would like to say otherwise, but we're circling. I'm going through the sex offenders. If anyone sticks out, they're sending the dogs to that property to sniff around."

"Can you do that without a search warrant?"

"I guess that's up for debate, but if a trooper just happens to be walking by with a dog and it alerts ... then we can get a search warrant. It's a vicious cycle."

"Well, at least it's something."

"Other than that, we've got nothing to go on. Mel is going through Jessica's phone records. There's a possibility she was involved in the kidnapping and her partner turned on her. There's also a chance she was killed as a distraction. We simply don't know which way it's leaning."

"I'm sorry." Harper meant it. "With your mother here, this is the worst time for things to go cold like this."

"My mother understands about being a cop. She also has you and Zander to entertain her."

"And we'll do that." Harper forced a smile. "Let me know if you need any help. Reading about sex offenders has to be better than putting sprinkles on cookies."

"Don't bet on that."

AN HOUR LATER, the kitchen crew had moved on to chocolate chip cookies that were making Jared's mouth water from afar as he waded through one horrific file after the other. He was bothered by the things he was reading, didn't want to allow horrible things like that in the home he shared with Harper, and yet he wanted to be close to the action. Therefore, he continued working in the living room. Even though he didn't add a lot to the conversation, he enjoyed watching Harper interact with his mother.

"How are you doing?" Harper asked as she delivered a mug of hot chocolate to him and perched on the arm of his chair to read over his shoulder.

"It's dull and disgusting work."

"I bet." Harper frowned as she read the file. "That guy raped his elderly neighbor."

Jared nodded. "She was ninety-five."

"How is he still alive?"

"You'll have to ask him. He only got seven years for it and is free.

However foul he is, though, he's not who we're looking for." Jared hit a button to go to the next file.

Curious despite herself, Harper tilted her head. "How do you know he's not the one you're looking for?"

"Because he committed rape as part of a home invasion scheme. He was mostly interested in robbing people. He's not a pedophile."

"Oh." Harper made a face. "You don't think Zoe was taken by a pedophile, do you?" The possibility was almost more than she could bear.

"I hope not. We simply don't know, Heart. This is the first time since I moved here where I wished Whisper Cove had more technology going for it. Other downtown areas have cameras at every corner. Not Whisper Cove. What happened that day outside the coffee shop couldn't have happened in other cities and towns."

"It could've happened," Harper countered. "You would simply have a lot more to go on."

"We would probably already have her back."

"Maybe. You don't know that, though."

"Yeah." He rubbed his forehead. "I guess I'm just feeling sorry for myself. The longer we go without finding her, the darker my thoughts get."

Harper could see that. "Listen … ." She grabbed the computer from his lap and moved it to the coffee table so she could take its spot. She slid close to him, tugging a blanket from the arm to cover them both and snuggled in close. "I think you're being too hard on yourself. There's no way you can singlehandedly solve this. We need a little help."

"And where do you suggest we get this help?" he asked, his hand moving over her back as he inhaled the scent of her. "You smell like vanilla, by the way."

"Zander put some behind my ears because he claims it's an aphrodisiac. Apparently he read in some magazine that men associate vanilla with cookies and that makes them happy … and horny. He said that in front of your mother, by the way."

"I can't argue with that." He kissed her cheek. "I do kind of want to … do this." He rubbed his nose against her neck, causing her to laugh. "Seriously. If you were a cookie, I would be dunking you in milk right about now."

"That is a really weird thing to say."

"It's also true."

"Yeah, well ... what was I saying again?"

"You were explaining that I'm taking things to heart too much, that I can't solve a mystery when I don't yet have enough clues, and that I'm the most handsomest man in the world."

"*I'm* the most handsomest man in the world," Zander corrected from the kitchen, causing them to look in his direction.

Pam, who was standing by the counter, smiled so broadly Harper was convinced her face might actually split in half. "You guys are so cute," she exclaimed, causing Shawn to smile and Zander to roll his eyes.

"They're not cute," Zander argued, wildly waving a spatula for emphasis. "They're annoying. Do you have any idea how frustrating it is to watch them paw each other every single day?"

"Well, that won't be an issue for much longer," Pam said pragmatically. "Harper and Jared have their own house. You guys are moving right after Christmas, right?"

Harper nodded as Zander's scowl deepened.

"I don't want Harper to move," he complained. "I think Jared should move over there and she should stay with me. She can visit him across the street and things will stay the same between us."

"I think you're worried that Jared is supplanting you in Harper's life," Pam noted, her smile soft as she patted Zander's arm. "You've been her closest confidant since you were children, and Jared's appearance in your life seems somehow threatening."

Zander's expression was withering. "I am not threatened."

"In your head, you're picturing a substantial shift occurring when Harper moves in with Jared," Pam continued, ignoring his petulance. "You think she's never going to visit because Jared will want to keep her close. I don't happen to believe that's reality."

"Oh, yeah?" Zander cocked an eyebrow. "You just met us. You don't know how things will go."

"Why don't you tell me how you think they'll go."

"I think that once they have their own place Harper is going to spend more and more time over there and then we'll suddenly turn into work acquaintances rather than friends."

"You don't really believe that." Pam was matter-of-fact. "You know that's a fabrication your mind has come up with because you're terrified of change. The thing is, change can be good or bad. You're assuming this change will be bad. What happens if things get even better?"

Suspicion lit Zander's eyes. "How are things going to get better?"

"Well, for starters, you're going to build a stronger relationship with Shawn," Pam explained. "Sharing a roof opens possibilities for a relationship. You and Shawn will be able to broaden your intimacy and set up boundaries for your own home. Jared and Harper will be able to do the same.

"It's not as if Harper is moving to another town," she continued. "In fact, she's not even moving across town. She'll be across the road. That seems to be a strategic move to me. Whoever thought of that was a genius."

Jared preened as Zander glared at him.

"I'm sure you know that moving across the road was your son's grand plan," Zander complained.

"I do know that," Pam confirmed, her lips twitching. "I'm sure if he had his druthers, he would've picked a house with a little more distance because you and he irritate each other. However, he had Harper's needs in mind when he selected it.

"He wanted what was best for all concerned parties," she continued. "That's why you guys are still going to be close but not on top of each other."

"I should've known you would take his side," Zander muttered.

"It's not about taking sides. It's about ... possibilities. You have a lot of possibilities with this set-up. Think about when you have children. They'll be able to race across the road to see each other and you won't have to worry, not like that poor child who is out there right now."

"Ugh." Zander's distaste was palpable. "You're basically telling me to stop being a baby and suck it up."

"Oh, look at that," Pam teased. "You do listen. I was starting to wonder."

"I don't find you all that charming any longer," Zander complained. "You've lost everything that made you a delight."

"You'll get over it." Pam wasn't the type to put up with Zander's shenanigans so she left him to pout in the kitchen and moved into the living room. "As for you, Jared, you're being a defeatist. I understand this particular case must be difficult — no one wants to think of a child being taken in this manner — but there has to be something you're missing. Nothing is unsolvable."

"We're doing the best we can," Jared said. "Right now, though, we don't know where to look. Going through the sex offenders is something that's necessary, but I don't think it's going to lead us to the right place."

"So ... what do you think is going to lead you to the right place?"

"If I knew that, I would be putting Zoe in her mother's arms right now."

"I think it's someone who wanted a child," Harper volunteered, drawing multiple sets of eyes to her. "I'm being serious. The more I think about it, the more I think we're dealing with a lost soul who was trying to make herself feel better by taking a child to love."

"You're assuming it's a woman," Jared pointed out. "Statistically, if what you're theorizing is true, then the numbers would hold that out. We simply have no proof of that, though."

"Is there a way to narrow down possible suspects?" Pam asked, getting into the spirit of the conversation. "I mean ... are there any mothers in the area who recently lost children? It probably doesn't even have to be by death. Maybe someone lost custody of a child."

"Or maybe someone splits custody of a child and the other parent has that specific child this holiday season and that caused the non-custodial parent to snap," Shawn suggested.

Jared jerked his head in Shawn's direction, intrigued. "Hmm. That right there is an angle that I didn't think about. Does anyone know a mother — or father, I guess, but it would probably most likely be a mother — who fits into any of those scenarios?"

"Um ... there's Denise Dixon," Harper offered after a beat. "She split with her husband last year. She had her daughter Kelsey last Christmas and her ex-husband has her this year. I know because I heard her complaining about it in the coffee shop about a week ago."

"That's good." In his haste to lean forward and reclaim his computer, Jared accidentally knocked Harper from her perch on his lap. "Sorry, Heart, but I need to make a list."

"No problem." She waved away the apology. "This is important. Who else can we think of?"

"Chris Butler comes into my gym all the time," Shawn volunteered. "He's been complaining that his ex-wife is taking their son to Hawaii this year so he won't even be able to see the kid. I know you think it's probably a woman — and I would guess that the child in question would probably be a girl — but you never know."

"That's good." Jared bobbed his head and typed information into his computer. "Who else?"

"There's Kasey Blankenship," Zander volunteered. "Her daughter died of cancer two years ago. It was two days before Christmas. Remember that, Harp?"

Harper's smile vanished as she nodded. "It was really sad. They thought they could get the little girl through her final Christmas, but it wasn't to be. The funeral was the day after Christmas, and it was basically the worst funeral I'd ever been to."

"What about Kasey now?" Jared asked. "Do you think she's moving on, or is she dwelling on the past?"

"Last time I checked, she was spending a lot of time at the bar," Zander replied. "I saw her there a few times when I was first meeting Shawn for drinks. She made me sad. That was months ago, though. I know the bartender was giving her a break on the drinks and arranged for an Uber to drive her home every night. He was essentially enabling her."

"That's probably not helpful," Jared noted. "That's a good lead, though. Anyone else?"

They spent the next hour coming up with names, which allowed Jared to send a list of addresses to the state police so they could search for signs of Zoe. Once the names were sent, it was a waiting game.

They didn't have enough evidence for formal searches and until they found something, they were dead in the water.

"Who wants to help me make roast beef for dinner?" Zander asked at some point.

"I think we should go out," Jared countered. "It's getting late, and Jason's restaurant is right down the road. I think it would be simpler."

"I don't want to go to Jason's restaurant. He's a thunder-stealer."

Pam snickered. "You have a problem with a lot of people, don't you?"

"It's all them, not me."

"I think we should talk about that."

Harper pursed her lips as she watched the scene and turned her attention to Jared. "What's the deal with your mother?" she whispered. "Why does she keep psychoanalyzing us?"

"She's a former social worker. Didn't I tell you that?"

"No, but it explains a lot."

"She was good at her job."

"She's driving Zander insane."

Jared beamed. "That's why I love her."

Sixteen

Pam was having a good time despite the heavy discussion occurring in the other room. Jared and Harper had their heads bent together, clearly intrigued at the prospect of following a thread that could possibly lead to Zoe being okay, and they seemed excited as they jotted down notes.

"They're cute, huh?" she mused to Zander and Shawn, who were helping her in the kitchen.

Shawn followed her gaze and smiled. "They're very cute," he agreed.

"I find them annoying," Zander countered.

Pam didn't take the comment to heart. "I think you're all talk."

Zander shook his head. "No, they're definitely annoying."

She snickered. "You crack me up." She wiped her hands on a towel and pinned him with a hard gaze so he had no chance to look elsewhere. "I also think you're exaggerating how you really feel because that's what you do."

Zander refused to back down. "No, I really find them annoying."

Pam let loose an exaggerated sigh. "You love Harper."

"Of course I love her. We've been best friends since we were kids. We've always been there for each other."

"You love Jared, too."

Zander worked his jaw. "I find Jared incredibly annoying," he said after a beat. "I know he's your son and you don't want to hear that, but he should honestly be smacked around he's so annoying."

Instead of being offended, Pam chuckled. "Oh, you're hilarious. You talk big, but you love them both."

"I believe you're mistaken," Zander said primly. "I love Harper and tolerate Jared."

"No, you love them both and put on a show because you have a certain reputation to uphold," she corrected. "I happen to know that you helped my son pick out a special gift for Harper this Christmas and he's very excited to put it to use."

Zander stilled, surprised. "W-what?"

"Oh, I see I've taken you off guard for the first time. That's kind of cute." Pam beamed as Shawn slid his boyfriend a sidelong look.

"Did you actually manage to finish picking out the gift before you got caught up in Zoe's disappearance?" Shawn asked. "I just realized I forgot to ask."

Zander sent a furtive look into the living room to make sure Harper and Jared were still caught up in each other and not listening. "Just ... shh." He pressed his fingers to his lips as he glared. "Are you trying to kill me with this? I mean ... seriously." His eyes flashed with annoyance. "It's a secret, and you're going to ruin it for Harper if you're not careful. If you do that, I don't care how much I like you, I'm going to be really angry."

Pam's smile only widened. "I have no intention of ruining it. Why would I want to ruin it?"

Zander held his hands palms out and shrugged. "I don't know. Some mothers — I'm not saying you, but *some* mothers — don't like it when their sons get married."

Shawn found himself unbelievably amused by Zander's reaction. "He got the ring, didn't he? Is it pretty? Do you know how he's going to propose?"

The look Zander shot him was withering. "Shut your hole. I will ... ." He trailed off and mimed strangling his boyfriend. He was so caught up in potential outrage that he didn't notice Harper and Jared were on their feet in the other room until he heard the door open. "Where are you going?" he called out, straightening.

Harper glanced over her shoulder. "We're going to Kasey Blankenship's house," she replied. "Jared finds her interesting enough to check out, and I'm going with him."

"Since when are you a police officer?"

"She's my civilian consultant," Jared corrected. "I'm allowed to utilize as many civilian consultants as I need."

"And what's her special ability in this particular case?"

"Kasey Blankenship lost a daughter," Jared replied simply. "Perhaps she's still around. Besides that, Jessica and Kasey went to high school together. It's a tenuous tie because I'm not sure if they were close after graduation, but it's enough that I want to question her."

"To what end?" Pam asked, legitimately curious. "Do you think she was working with Jessica?"

"Maybe." Jared saw no reason to lie. "I mean ... think about it. Maybe Jessica wanted to get rid of Zoe as a way to eliminate one of the ties between Ally and Luke. Perhaps she didn't want to kill her, though. She knew Kasey wanted a daughter and was potentially sad enough to join in the plot so they hatched the plan as a duo."

"Then why kill Jessica?" Shawn asked. "Why not stick to the original plan?"

"Perhaps Jessica changed her mind and wanted to take Zoe back to her mother," Harper suggested. "Maybe she didn't realize how much attention the abduction would garner. Maybe she felt bad for what she did and wanted to make it right."

"And maybe Kasey didn't want her to make it right," Jared added as he grabbed a hat from the hook and pulled it over Harper's head, making sure her ears were covered. "Maybe Kasey wanted to keep Zoe no matter what."

"It sounds like you're reaching to me," Zander argued.

"We're still going to head over there. Mom, will you be okay staying here with Zander and Shawn?"

Pam nodded without hesitation. "Absolutely. I'm looking forward to it."

Momentarily suspicious, Jared narrowed his eyes. "What are you guys going to do while we're gone?"

"We're going to make dinner so you have something wonderful and tasty to return home to," Pam replied smoothly. "I would think you'd be happy about that."

"I guess it depends what you're cooking."

"I was leaning toward pot roast."

Jared brightened considerably. "I love pot roast."

"I know." Pam's smile was fond. "We'll make dinner. You guys take your time and be careful."

"And keep us updated," Shawn called out.

"We'll definitely do that."

Pam waited until Jared and Harper were safely out of the house before turning to Zander. "Now you have no reason to be fussy and obnoxious," she noted. "Why don't you tell me exactly what the ring looks like, huh? In fact, if you know where it's hidden, that would be even better."

Zander's expression darkened. "I thought we were making pot roast."

"I can multitask. I want to see the ring."

"And I want to know how you managed to keep this a secret from me," Shawn added. "You can never keep secrets. Yes, I know I forgot to ask when things blew up, but this is something you should've told me about. I simply assumed you didn't have time to buy the ring after all."

Zander balked. "Excuse me. I'll have you know that I'm an excellent secret keeper."

"You're the absolute worst. I can't believe Jared trusted you instead of me."

"He trusted Zander because he wanted to make sure Harper got the ring of her dreams," Pam supplied. "I know my son. Ring shopping wouldn't be high on his talent list. Zander, however, knows Harper better than anyone."

"Did he get her a nice ring?" Shawn asked. "Wait!" He held up his hand. "This is more important. When and where is he going to propose?"

"It's going to be a Christmas proposal," Zander replied. "He hasn't told me all the details."

"Oh, please." Shawn rolled his eyes. "I know you. There's no way you would've let him leave without ferreting out the details."

"We were barely out of the store when Ally started screaming about Zoe being missing."

"Oh." Realization dawned on Shawn's face. "I guess that's a good reason for losing your train of thought."

"And he's been really busy since. There's been no opportunity to get him alone to ask questions about his plans. Harper has been with him pretty much every second that he's in this house."

"Well, we'll figure out the proposal going forward," Shawn said. "Show us the ring."

Pam nodded enthusiastically. "Definitely show us the ring."

Zander heaved out an exaggerated sigh. "People say I'm the one who can't mind my own business, but I think you guys are worse."

"I'm a mother," Pam noted. "I'm allowed to be a busybody. In fact, it's part of the rules."

Zander smirked. "Good point. I'll see if I can find the ring. You guys watch the windows to make sure Harper and Jared don't swing back while I'm going through their things. That would be annoying to explain."

"I'm on it." Shawn strode toward the window. "I can't believe you were going to keep this from me," he lamented. "I like proposals, too."

"I'll never make that mistake again. I promise."

JARED PARKED IN FRONT of the nondescript ranch house and killed the engine of his truck. He was using his personal vehicle because he didn't want to waste time returning to the office to claim a cruiser.

"How well do you know Kasey?" he asked Harper as he unbuckled his seatbelt.

"Not well. We were all in high school together, but they hung out with a different crowd. Ally and Jessica were popular. Zander and I were not. We were fine being in our own little group, though."

"Fair enough." He kept Harper close as he took the lead position to knock on the door.

Kasey answered right away — almost as if she was expecting someone — and she seemed surprised when she recognized the duo on her front porch. "Um ... hello."

"Hello." Jared pasted a friendly smile on his face. "I'm Detective Monroe with the Whisper Cove Police Department." He moved to reach in his pocket to retrieve his badge, but she waved him off.

"I know who you are," Kasey said. "You were big news in the spring when you showed up on the scene. Everyone wanted to get a look at you. Harper managed to snag you before anyone else could make a move, though."

Harper offered a half-smile, although she wasn't sure if she liked being talked about in such a fashion. "I don't know that I *snagged* him up," she hedged, causing Kasey to chuckle.

"It ultimately doesn't matter," she said. "You guys are clearly happy, and I'm happy for you. I'm not quite sure why you're here, though."

"We have a few questions that might seem odd," Jared admitted, shifting from one foot to the other. The air outside was biting. "They revolve around Jessica Hayden and the disappearance of Zoe Mathers."

Kasey's eyes widened. "Oh, well ... come in." She ushered them inside, waiting until they were over the threshold and finished removing their boots to lead them through the house. "Come into the living room," she suggested. "I have a fire brewing."

"It's really cold out," Harper noted, her mittens in her hand as she wandered into the cute living room and pulled up short.

There was a bottle of wine and two glasses on the table, a platter of cheese and crackers not far away. The lighting was low, atmosphere light, and there was soft music playing from the speaker on a nearby shelf.

"You have a date," Harper blurted out before thinking.

Kasey nodded, her cheeks flushing with color. "Dave Thompkins. Um ... we've been seeing each other a few weeks."

"I didn't know that." Harper glanced around, her stomach twisting as her eyes fell on a photograph on the mantel. It featured a young girl, her black hair flying as she smiled at the camera. She looked alive, happy, and about to get into mischief.

"Is that your daughter?" Jared asked, looking at the photograph over Harper's shoulder.

Kasey nodded, her expression turning sad. "Piper. Her name was Piper."

"Harper told me what happened." Jared chose his words carefully. "Leukemia, right?"

"Yes." Kasey's voice was soft as she stared at the photo. "She was a good girl. The best, really. She made my life better."

Harper's eyes burned thanks to the tortured look on Kasey's face. "She's been gone almost two years now, right? It was right around Christmas."

"Yeah." Kasey licked her lips and took a moment to pull herself together. "I kept telling myself she had to make it through Christmas because ... well, I had no idea why. Christmas was an arbitrary date set in my mind. It didn't matter if she made it to Christmas. My world was still going to be shattered when I lost her no matter what."

Jared did his best not to let the sympathy overcome him as he sat on the couch. "We don't want to take up a lot of your time. I understand you have a date."

"Dave is the first person I've spent time with since it happened," Kasey explained. "Mike and I never got married, and he visited Piper on alternating weekends after we broke up. When she died, I didn't think I ever wanted to date again. Dave changed that.

"I kept running into him, like it was meant to be or something, and we got to talking," she continued. "The next thing I knew, he was asking me out. My initial inclination was to say no, but then I thought about Piper. She wouldn't want me to be sad."

"She definitely wouldn't want that," Harper agreed. "I remember talking to her at a festival one year. It was a Halloween festival, because the kids were all over me for ghost stories. Anyway, she didn't want to hear about ghosts. She wanted to know if Zander and I were going to get married. She seemed keen on it."

"She always had a crush on Zander," Kasey supplied, grinning. "I tried explaining why it would never work between them, but she didn't get it. She wasn't old enough to get it. Then she got sick and it didn't seem to matter. Although ... Zander was so sweet. He stopped by the hospital and saw her three times during her last big stay. He was wonderful."

Harper was taken aback. "I didn't know that."

"He stopped between jobs or something. He always brought her a gift. I think he knew she had a crush on him."

"He never told me." Harper adopted a far-off expression as she thought about it and then shook her head to dislodge the melancholy. She had plenty of time to question Zander about his actions later. For now, they had to get through this. "I know this might sound like an odd question, but did you spend any time with Jessica Hayden?"

"No. You mentioned her on the porch, but Jessica and I weren't close. I mean ... we would wave to each other if we crossed paths. We weren't unfriendly. We stopped being true friends after graduation, though."

"So, you haven't spent any time with her over the past few months?" Jared queried.

Kasey shook her head. "No. Is there a reason you suspected I might be spending time with her?"

"She's dead," Harper volunteered, ignoring the incredulous look Jared shot her. "We found her in the park. Zoe Mathers's hat was in her car."

"What?" Kasey was shaking as she sat down in the chair across from the couch. "You think Jessica kidnapped Zoe?"

"Either that or someone wanted us to believe she did," Jared replied. "We're trying to track down every possible angle, including parents who lost children who might be feeling lonely this holiday season." He blurted it out, feeling like an idiot when her gaze sharpened. "I'm sorry. We just needed to check, and since you went to high school with Jessica ... ."

"You had to make sure," Kasey finished his sentence, no signs of anger crossing her pretty features. "I get it. If my child was missing, I would want you to follow every lead, however weak. You can search the house if you want. I don't have her. I wouldn't take her."

"It's not that we thought you would take her out of malice," Harper offered hurriedly. "It's just ... we thought you might be sad." She inclined her chin toward the wine glasses. "You're moving on, though. That's good."

"I don't know that I would say I'm moving on."

"You're dating. That's kind of like moving on."

"I'll never forget, or stop asking myself if there was something I could've done to save her. I'll never look at a Christmas tree and not wonder what she would be like this year, how she would've grown and matured if she'd lived. I'll never be able to put that behind me.

"Still, I can't spend my entire life shutting myself away from the world," she continued. "I have to either move forward or live in the past for the rest of my life. I seriously considered living in the past before I sucked it up and realized that I wasn't doing anyone any favors.

"I can't bring Piper back," she said. "I'm also not done living my life, so I have to force myself to move forward. I'll never let her go, though. She'll always be part of whatever life I decide to lead. Her memory looms large in my heart."

"I think that's a smart choice," Harper said. "It sounds like you've been giving it a lot of thought."

"Actually, I got that from my support group." Kasey was rueful. "I would like to take responsibility for coming to this conclusion myself, but they're the ones who pushed me. They're the ones giving me strength."

"There's no shame in that." Harper was firm. "If the group helps, that's all that matters. That's the same group Shana is part of, right? I believe she founded it."

"She didn't found it, although she claims responsibility for it," Kasey countered. "She was also kicked out of the group a few months ago. We couldn't take her crap any longer."

"What crap?" Jared asked.

"She's totally crazy. In fact, I think she's mentally ill. We couldn't trust her, so we had to cut her loose."

"Why couldn't you trust her?"

"Because she was coming up with some ridiculous ideas, like

removing kids from homes ourselves if we deem the parents aren't paying enough attention to the kids. It was totally wacky stuff."

Harper and Jared exchanged a weighted look.

"Tell me about it," Jared said finally. "And, please, don't leave anything out."

Seventeen

"She's just ... mental," Kasey explained. If she thought it was weird for Jared and Harper to change the topic of conversation to Shana, she didn't show it. "I mean, she's all over the place. It was supposed to be a group where everyone got to talk about losing their child, but she took over each and every time, to the point where no one else could get a word in edgewise."

"What kind of group was it?" Jared asked.

"It's for bereaved parents. The only stipulation for membership is losing a child. It doesn't matter if the child was murdered, died of natural causes, or was an adult when they passed."

"And Shana took over the group?" Harper pressed.

Kasey nodded. "I think it must have been legitimately harder for her because Chloe disappeared and there's no way of knowing what happened to her. Her membership wasn't initially a problem because odds are Chloe is dead, and Shana has obviously grieved. She made it a problem, though."

"Can you expand on that?" Jared prodded.

"I guess. Basically, she made everything about her. She told Chloe's story over and over, which is normal, but she refused to let others talk. She basically acted as if she was the only one suffering.

"In addition to that, she lied all the time," she continued. "She told wild stories about the FBI wanting to recruit her to be a profiler because she knew a lot about the criminal mind thanks to Chloe's disappearance. Of course, that didn't make any sense.

"That was on top of the fact that she would melt down if people didn't give her constant praise," she said. "When she would bring cookies to our meetings, she would get upset if people didn't tell her how good they were. One time, Helen Moffet brought cookies and everyone raved about them and Shana basically melted down."

Harper pursed her lips. "Did anyone ever call her on her behavior?"

"A few of us did. That just made things worse. She accused us of being jealous and painted herself as a victim. It got to be more and more uncomfortable, to the point where no one wanted to keep attending group if she was going to be part of it."

"She sounds like she has Narcissistic Personality Disorder," Jared mused, stroking his chin.

"You're not the first person who has said that," Shana admitted. "We have a therapist in the group and that's exactly what she said."

"How did Shana take it when you booted her from the group?" Jared asked, his mind racing. "And go back to that thing where she had the idea of stealing children."

"Well, that was essentially the last straw," Kasey admitted. "She put together folders for everyone — I'm not kidding — and they were basically how-to guides for identifying children who were being neglected.

"The thing is, she seemed to think a child was being neglected if he or she went to the park without a parent — we're talking about ten-year-olds here — or if a child played in a yard alone," she continued. "The things in that packet were outrageous."

"I'm assuming you called her on it," Jared prodded.

Kasey bobbed her head. "Of course we did. No one was going to agree to kidnap children. She said it wasn't kidnapping, rather that it was saving the children. She got really weird, to the point where we simply asked her to leave because we were uncomfortable."

"And how did she take that?"

"She freaked out. She said we couldn't have the group without her because she founded it. That wasn't true, by the way. The group was in operation years before she joined. She said that we couldn't keep her group and that we were trying to steal from her and stealing wasn't allowed. She was ranting and raving so loudly I thought someone would call the police."

"How did that end?" Harper asked.

"She basically stormed out of the group when she realized we weren't going to change our minds," Kasey replied. "She hasn't spoken to any of us since, at least to my knowledge."

"Well, that's interesting," Jared mused.

"Especially since she said she was working on behalf of a support group when she started hanging around Ally," Harper added, earning a curious stare from Jared. "That's what Ally told me. In fact, Ally also told me that Shana was telling her to let Zoe go even though she's only been missing for a few days."

"You didn't mention that," Jared said. "Why didn't you tell me about that?"

"Because Ally is messed up, and when I asked Shana about it, she said that wasn't remotely what she said to Ally," Harper replied. "How was I to know that Shana was probably lying? I don't know her all that well and she seemed perfectly rational."

"What if she's not, though?" Jared was thoughtful as he got to his feet. "What if Shana is the one who took Zoe? She might've made an enticing target because she was alone in front of the coffee shop."

"Still, that was a gutsy move," Harper argued. "She could've been caught."

"Maybe she didn't care in the moment. Maybe she decided that she needed a child to take the place of her lost one and Zoe fit the bill."

Kasey held up her hand to get their attention. "Listen, I don't want to get Shana in trouble if she's innocent or anything. I feel kind of bad that you're looking at her."

"You won't feel bad if we find Zoe and she's okay," Jared said, gesturing for Harper to move toward the door. "We thank you very much for your time, Kasey. We're sorry for bothering you. Have a good time on your date."

Kasey was incredulous. “That’s it? You’re not going to tell me what’s going on?”

“We don’t know what’s going on yet,” Harper replied as Kasey followed them to the front door. “You might have given us a very valuable clue, though. You have no idea how thankful we are for it.”

“Okay, well, keep me posted.”

“We’ll definitely do that,” Jared promised. “You’ve earned an update or two.”

THE HOUSE WAS BUZZING with activity when Jared and Harper returned. At first, because they weren’t gone very long everyone was upset. They assumed the trip had been a waste of time. Then Harper explained what Kasey had told them about Shana, and the entire room broke into pandemonium.

“You can’t be serious.” Zander was aghast. “You think Shana is behind it? But ... she’s like the go-to person for missing children in the area. She can’t be a kidnapper.”

“Maybe that’s exactly why she’s a kidnapper,” Jared offered, grabbing his phone from his pocket and striding toward the bedroom. “I’m going to try and get a warrant. Fill them in, Heart. Hopefully we’ll be able to move on this tonight.”

Harper nodded as she watched him go, thoughtful.

“He calls you ‘Heart,’ huh?” Pam’s amusement was obvious. “I thought I heard him say it earlier, but I wasn’t sure because we were in the restaurant and everyone was talking at once. That is the most adorable thing ever.”

Harper’s cheeks burned under Pam’s scrutiny. “It’s just something he started doing.”

“That made Harper go gushy,” Zander teased, poking her stomach before sobering. “Seriously, though, do you really think it could be Shana?”

Harper held her hands palms out and shrugged. “I don’t know. I’ve always thought she was a little off, but I convinced myself it was because she was trapped in a state of perpetual grief. The things Kasey told us were ... weird.”

For lack of anything better to do, Harper launched into the tale. When she was done, everyone was rapt.

"Wow," Shawn said finally. "That sounds odd. Did you know that about her? I mean ... that she was a narcissist."

"I don't know her well enough to make a clinical diagnosis," Harper replied drily. "Seriously, I've only ever seen her around town and at gatherings. I've barely talked to her. Although ... ." She trailed off, something occurring to her.

"I know exactly what you're thinking," Zander surmised. "She came around after Quinn disappeared. She wanted to sit with you, offer prayers and a shoulder to cry on. You were a mess and your mother chased her away.

"We weren't living in this house at the time," he continued. "We were in apartments. We didn't move in together until months later, when I was certain you wouldn't come out of your funk without an intervention."

"And you definitely got me out of my funk." Harper graced him with a heartfelt smile. "You were the one who saved me from the self-doubt."

"Yes, I'm a hero," Zander agreed. "I remember thinking it was weird the night Shana showed up, though. Quinn wasn't your child, so I didn't know how she expected to help. She kept claiming she had expertise to give. I was so worried about you, though, that I couldn't focus on her. Now I'm suspicious."

"Yes, well, that makes two of us." Harper chewed on her bottom lip. "Shana went out of her way to 'help' Ally. She told her to move on. When I questioned her about saying that to Ally, she denied it, said Ally was making it up. What if Ally wasn't making it up, though? What if that's part of Shana's game?"

"How would that be part of it?" Shawn asked.

"If Shana really is a narcissist — and from the things Kasey said, it sounds entirely possible — then she would get off on manipulating the emotions of others," Harper explained. "I'm not an expert on personality disorders, but narcissism is an ugly one. Shana is definitely an attention whore."

"I always thought she was that way because she needed a hard outer shell to ease the pain she was feeling inside," Zander said. "Maybe it started that way and she somehow turned into another person. I mean ... people do strange things when they're grieving, right?"

Harper nodded, her mind busy. "I can't remember her before Chloe disappeared. I just remember seeing her everywhere — on television, in the newspapers, on the radio — in the aftermath. Chloe's disappearance shook everyone because, before that, we assumed Whisper Cove was a safe place."

"Whisper Cove *is* a safe place," Zander said. "No place is without danger, though. That's impossible in this day and age."

"I think it was always impossible," Shawn offered. "We just didn't hear the stories back in the day because there was no internet to disseminate them."

"That's probably true," Pam agreed. "Do you think Jared will get a warrant?"

Jared returned from the bedroom before Harper could answer and she turned to him with hope in her eyes. It was quickly dashed.

"The judge says we don't have enough for a warrant," Jared volunteered, grim. "I tried arguing with him, explaining the nature of the situation, but we need more to go on."

"So, what are you going to do?" Harper asked.

"I'm going to stakeout Shana's home. Maybe I'll be able to see Zoe through the window or something. That would be enough to enter the house without a warrant. It would be just cause."

"Do you think she would be stupid enough to allow Zoe near the windows?"

"No, but I can't do nothing."

Harper took in the serious set of his jaw and nodded. "Well, then I'll go with you."

"No." He immediately began shaking his head. "That's not necessary. It's cold out. I'll be there half the night. Mel is going to relieve me after midnight."

"I want to be with you." Harper was firm. "Zander and Shawn will entertain your mother and make sure there's pot roast for us when we get back. Isn't that right?"

"I guess." Zander didn't look thrilled with the prospect. "I think you should stay here with us and eat the pot roast now. You're not a cop."

"No, but maybe Jessica will be at Shana's house," Harper pointed out. "Maybe she'll remember what happened to her and give us something that leads to the evidence we need. That's a chance I'm not willing to pass up."

Zander let loose an exaggerated sigh. "Fine. I'll save some pot roast for you. Just make sure you actually watch the house for signs of Zoe and don't spend the entire night fogging up the windows."

"Why would you care how foggy the windows get?" Jared asked.

"Because car sex is gauche."

Jared smirked. "Good to know. I don't think you have to worry about that, though. I'm determined to find Zoe before Christmas. This just ... feels right. I think we're going to find the answers we need this time."

Harper hoped he was right.

"I'VE NEVER BEEN ON a stakeout before," Harper said as she glanced out the window and stared at Shana's house. Jared picked a spot on the street that was hidden by a thick cropping of trees. They could see the windows of the house clearly, but it would be difficult for Shana to see them thanks to the darkness.

"What are you supposed to do on a stakeout?" Harper asked.

Jared snickered. "You're supposed to sit quietly and watch the suspect for signs of suspicious activity."

"We don't even know our suspect is home," Harper pointed out. "I mean ... the lights are on, but that doesn't necessarily mean anything."

As if on cue, a shadowy figure moved past the nearest window. It definitely belonged to an adult, which was something of a bummer for Jared, but he straightened as he watched the shadow move toward what looked to be a stove.

"Her windows have some sort of protective coating on them or something," he complained. "It makes seeing inside difficult."

"We could always sneak up to the house and get a closer look."

"Not legally."

"Okay, well … ." Harper tapped her bottom lip and shifted gears. "I could sneak up to the house and look through the windows. You're a police officer. You can't break the law. I'm a rule breaker so I can do whatever I want."

Jared rolled his eyes. "If I see you breaking the law, I have to arrest you."

"That's not what you said when you grabbed my butt on Main Street last week. You could've been arrested for lewd and lascivious acts for that one."

Jared narrowed his eyes to dangerous slits. "That was an accident. I reached lower than I meant to. I was trying to hug you."

"Right. You were still breaking public decency laws. When I mentioned it, you said no one saw so it wasn't a big deal."

"I wish you would stop bringing things up that I say when I'm trying to get away with something."

Harper snickered, genuinely amused. "So … do you want me to sneak closer and get a better look?"

Despite his law-and-order attitude, Jared honestly considered it. Ultimately, though, he shook his head. "Not yet. Let's watch for a little bit before I okay you breaking the law. I would prefer to handle this by the book."

"Such a cop." Harper leaned over and kissed him, her eyes sparkling. "This is fun, huh? We've never been on a stakeout together before."

Jared grabbed the thermos of coffee his mother packed before they left the house and twisted off the top. "You get excited over the oddest things. Has anyone ever told you that?"

She shook her head. "I've been excited about you since the moment we met. I didn't want to tell you that, of course, because I had a reputation to uphold, but I've always been infatuated with you."

His heart simply melted. "I felt the same way about you."

"You thought I was a quack."

"I thought you were the most beautiful woman I'd ever seen in real life. I still think that. Sometimes, when I wake up before you, I watch you sleep and marvel that you're mine."

Harper was absurdly touched by the words. "I feel the same way."

He gently slipped a strand of hair behind her ear before pouring coffee into the thermos cap and handing it to her. "I love you, Heart. You can't serve as a distraction tonight, though. We actually have to be diligent and watch the house. No fogging up the windows, as Zander would say."

Harper giggled as she sipped the caffeinated goodness. "I'll try to refrain from ripping your clothes off."

"That's only a rule while we're on the stakeout. Once we get home, you can resume all bad behavior."

"I'll keep that in mind."

Eighteen

Under different circumstances, Harper and Jared might have enjoyed their time together. They talked, Harper asking questions about Jared's childhood and him responding with anecdotes that made her giggle.

When the temperature dropped low, rather than start the engine and warm up the truck – which would've potentially drawn attention to them – they snuggled closer. Harper rested her head on Jared's shoulder and they shared each other's warmth. Harper almost dropped off, in fact, was just on the cusp, when there was a loud knock on the window that almost caused her to jump out of her skin.

Even Jared, who was usually calm under pressure, jerked so hard he slammed his chin against Harper's head.

"Ow!"

On the other side of the window, Mel hunkered down with his hands on his knees and laughed at the scene.

"That's what you get for groping on the job," Mel said.

"Shh." Jared pressed his finger to his lips and turned the key far enough to engage the battery and roll down the window. "Don't yell," he hissed. "Voices carry when it's cold like this."

"The lights are out." Mel inclined his chin toward the house. "Did you miss that?"

Jared made a face. The last thing he wanted to admit was that he'd become distracted when he was supposed to be working. "I ... it must have just happened."

"Yeah, it happened when you kissed her forehead and readjusted to make sure she was snuggled as closely as possible. I've been here for five minutes. I've been watching both of you."

"Ugh." Jared spared a glance for Harper and found her smiling. "You think this is funny, huh?"

"I think we would both fail as spies."

"I can live with that." He gave her a quick kiss before fixing his full attention on Mel. "You're early. How come?"

"Because I thought maybe we could do a quick perimeter check of the house together once the lights were off."

Jared was convinced he'd misheard his partner. "On what grounds?"

"On the grounds that a little girl is missing and this is literally the only thing we've got to go on. Tomorrow is Christmas Eve. I can't be the only one who wants that little girl home with her mother."

"No." Jared shifted back to Harper. "Are you okay if I leave you here to do a search with Mel?"

Harper nodded without hesitation. "Go. I'll stay here."

"I'll start the engine so you can warm up." He reached for the key but she stopped him.

"No. You're right about that drawing attention to us. Go with Mel. I'll be fine. I'm in no danger of freezing to death."

"Are you sure?"

"I'm sure. I'll be fine."

"Okay." He gave her another kiss. "I'll be right back. It shouldn't take us long."

"I'll be waiting with Christmas bells on."

"Ho, ho, ho."

HARPER WASN'T THE nervous sort. Most people left alone in the middle of the night, surrounded by trees and looking for a kidnapper, would've been antsy. That wasn't how she operated. She recognized ghosts, talked to them, and understood that they weren't to be feared ... except for the occasionally nutty one that had been alone so long it had gone around the bend. She'd faced down death more times than she could count. Fear very rarely got a foothold in her world.

Despite that, an eerie sense of dread settled over her as she watched the darkness for hints of movement. Mel and Jared disappeared to the east, but her eyes kept darting to the west for some reason. It wasn't that she necessarily saw movement as much as it was an inner feeling.

Some thing wanted her to look in that direction.

No, not some *thing*. Someone.

Before she even realized what she was doing, Harper pushed open the passenger side door and climbed out. Her hat was blue, so it covered up a decent amount of her blond hair as she zipped her coat and took two steps forward.

"Hello?" Her voice was barely a whisper. "Is someone out there?"

She waited so long, staring into nothing, that she convinced herself that she had imagined the previous feeling that overtook her. She was close to turning around and climbing back into the truck when the sensation that she was being watched barreled into her with enough force that she almost toppled over.

She slowly adjusted her sightline to the left, her heart dropping through her feet when she caught sight of the ghost. At first, for one fleeting second, she thought it was Jessica. She hadn't seen the recently-murdered woman since their previous interaction – and she was starting to get worried – but hers wasn't the face staring back at Harper this evening. No, the girl looking at Harper was from the past.

"Chloe." Harper couldn't believe her eyes. "What are you doing here?"

The ghost looked exactly like she had in life. She was a lovely girl, a teenager who would've one day grown into a knockout of a woman. She wore jeans and a simple T-shirt, a spring jacket instead of a winter coat. Her long hair was in disarray, and her makeup was smeared halfway down her face. Clearly, in death, Chloe never learned that she could change her appearance. Now, years later, she looked exactly like she had when she shuffled off the mortal coil.

"I can't believe you're here." Harper felt like an idiot as she stared at the ghost. "I never thought to look for you. If I'd known ... I mean, have you been here since you died?"

Chloe nodded, her eyes roaming Harper's features. "You look familiar to me," she said finally. "I don't recognize you, and yet I do. It's a very weird feeling."

"My name is Harper Harlow. I was behind you in school."

"Behind me?" She looked Harper up and down. "You're older than me."

"You've been dead a long time."

"I guess so. It felt like a long time, but I couldn't be sure. I don't know how to explain it."

"That's okay." Harper flashed an understanding smile. "I'm so sorry that I didn't know you were out here. I would've come if I'd known. I would've helped you cross over."

"To where?"

"To the other side. I don't know what's over there, but I've seen glimpses a few times. It's beautiful."

"And you can help me cross over?"

"I can."

"That would be nice." Chloe brightened a bit, although she hardly looked happy. "It's not time for that yet, though."

"No?"

"No. I have something I have to show you."

"You have something you have to show me?" Harper was understandably confused. "Where?"

"This way." Chloe beckoned and started moving toward the trees.

"I have to wait," Harper called out, jerking her head to the east in the hope she would catch sight of Jared or Mel. Unfortunately, it was dark and silent.

"You can't wait. There is no time to wait. You have to come."

"But ... why?"

"Because it's going to happen again if you don't save her."

"What's going to happen again?"

"My mother will win."

Harper was unbelievably confused but something inside propelled her forward. Since she wasn't an idiot, though, she held up her hand and tugged off her mitten. "Hold on. I have to leave Jared a note."

She didn't have paper or a pen, but she had the condensation on the window that still lingered. She opened the door, breathed hard to increase the fog, and left Jared a simple message. "Ghost came. Went into woods. Be right back."

Harper read the note, scanned the woods surrounding the house again, and then shut the door. She wasn't going far. She was certain of that. She would be fine. Chloe clearly had answers, and Harper was more than ready to hear them.

THE WALK INTO THE woods took longer than Harper envisioned. To be fair, they didn't go far. It only felt that way because Harper had to walk slowly to make sure she didn't accidentally trip over a fallen branch and bang her head into an unforeseen barrier.

Chloe wasn't much for talk and she remained far enough ahead of Harper that the blonde felt it unwise to call out and draw her back. Finally, when Harper thought she could take it no longer, Chloe circled behind a thick crop of trees and disappeared.

Harper increased her pace and pulled up short when she realized she was looking at a small building that was completely shrouded by trees.

"What the ... ?"

"It's the quiet place," Chloe whispered, something about her tone causing Harper to snap her head in the young girl's direction.

"The quiet place?"

Chloe nodded. "Mother likes it quiet." The words were barely a whisper and they sent a shiver down Harper's spine.

"Oh, Chloe, did your mother kill you?" Harper blurted out the question without giving it much thought.

Instead of balking, Chloe merely nodded. "I wasn't quiet enough, good enough. I knew better than mouthing off, but I thought I caught her in a good mood. I wanted to go to prom, you see. She always told me that was for girls who didn't want good things for their future, sluts. She chaperoned the homecoming dances, but she made sure I never got too close to anybody. The prom was a different story. I wasn't to bother her, but Rodney Daughtry asked me, and I wanted to go."

Harper felt sick to her stomach. "Your mother killed you, reported you missing, and then spent fifteen years playing the victim. I can't believe it. How did she pull it off?"

"Look."

"She fooled everyone," Harper barreled forward, not noticing the way Chloe gestured at the building. "She had every single person in this town feeling sorry for her and she was the one who killed you. I can't believe it."

She swiveled and pinned Chloe with a dark look. "Tell me how she killed you. I can't help unless you tell me where your body is. We'll nail her. I promise. We'll make sure she pays for what she did to you."

"Look," Chloe repeated, her fingers going close to the small outbuilding's door. "Look."

A wave of nausea washed over Harper. "Oh. You brought me out here because you wanted me to find you."

Chloe nodded. "You have to look. Then it will be real."

Harper wasn't sure what to make of the statement, but she did as she was asked. She wrapped her mitten-covered hand around the handle and gave it a tug. It held tight, so she had to try again. Finally, she had to brace her feet and put her back into it. When the door flew open, Harper lost her balance and toppled backward.

The ground was cold when she hit, and her hip groaned in protest because the frozen surface offered zero cushion. "Ow." Harper made a face as she rubbed her hip, glaring into the dark opening.

There were no streetlights in the area, but the moon managed to filter through the bare branches and give Harper a relatively good view of what was inside the shed.

There was nothing left of Chloe, at least nothing identifiable. Her skull remained, empty black eyeholes staring into the darkness. Clothes that looked eerily familiar because the ghost wore the same outfit that was on the floor, although they were old and had seen better days. There was also hair, although it was nowhere near as glossy and pretty as Harper remembered from her youth.

"Did you die in there?" Harper remained on the ground, her sore hip forgotten. "Did your mother kill you in there?"

"That was where I lived when she needed quiet," Chloe explained. "She doesn't like noise. Never liked it. I learned quickly as a child, although not quickly enough." She held up her ghostly hand so Harper could see how the pinkie and ring fingers on her left hand weren't perfectly straight. "You have to be careful and not make noise."

"She hurt you." It was a statement, not a question. "She hurt you when you were little. Didn't your father say something?" Now that she asked the question, Harper realized that she couldn't remember Shana ever being married. "Wait ... what happened to your father?"

"He left when I was three. I don't remember him."

"I'm sorry." Harper meant it. "No one should have to go through what you went through. Did you ever try telling someone? Maybe a teacher or a family friend."

"Who would've believed me?"

"I would have."

"Weren't you a child, too?"

"Yes, but I meant that I would've believed whatever you told me so there had to be other adults around at the time who would've believed it, too."

"Does it really matter?" Chloe was obviously defeated. "It's too late for me."

Harper pursed her lips. "It matters to me. What happened to you? You said you asked her to go to the prom. I'm guessing that didn't go over well."

"Only whores want to go to prom," Chloe said. "I shouldn't have asked. I knew better. My hopes were greater than my brains that day, though. She yelled ... and screamed ... and hit me with the pan on the counter. She was making dinner, and she hates being interrupted when she's making dinner.

"I woke up in the quiet place after that," she continued. "My head hurt, and there was blood in my hair ... and in my ears ... and in my mouth. It hurt everywhere. In fact, it hurt so much I almost wished I didn't wake up.

"I waited for her to come and get me like she usually did," she said. "She would give me a chance to apologize. The key was not to apologize for the first go around, because she never believed it anyway. You had to wait for the second or third time, depending on the infraction, to make her believe it.

"She never came this time, though," she said, her face twisting. "The pain got really bad ... and then it wasn't so bad. That was the scariest part. I knew when it stopped hurting that something was wrong inside of my head. That when I closed my eyes again, they would never open.

"I tried to hang on, but it was impossible. Eventually, I could no longer keep my eyes open. I drifted away, into the best sleep of my life, and woke up in this place all over again."

Harper wanted to hug the ghost, offer some sort of comfort. She couldn't, though. There was nothing she could give Chloe but a promise that her mother wouldn't walk free another day.

"I can help you, Chloe. I can ... help you move on. You don't have to stay here. You can celebrate Christmas this year on the other side. In fact, I don't have a dreamcatcher with me right now, but I can go home and get one. I can be back here and help you cross over within the hour."

Chloe forced a smile, but it was wan. "I can't leave yet. I have one more thing to do."

"If you want to make your mother pay, I can guarantee that she'll be behind bars before the end of the night. Those two men I was with earlier, they're police detectives. They'll help me. All we have to do is show them this and I guarantee they'll drag your mother out of bed and she'll be finished."

"I have a feeling my mother is going to face more than one sort of judge," Chloe said. "I'm not worried about that. This isn't about her. It's about the other girl."

"What other girl?"

"The little girl."

Realization dawned on Harper and she remembered why she was

really in the woods that night. “Zoe.” The name came out on a half-gasp. “Your mother has Zoe, doesn’t she? Oh, my ... .” Harper jerked her head back in the direction they came from. “We have to go back.”

“You see, right?” Chloe was insistent. “You see what she is. That little girl doesn’t see. She doesn’t know the rules. You have to get her tonight.”

“Oh, I’m going to get her.” Harper squared her shoulders in determination as she regained her footing and began walking, ignoring the pain shooting through hip as she increased her pace. “We’re going to get her right now, Chloe. Come on. You won’t want to miss what’s about to happen. Your mother is finally going to get what’s coming to her.”

Nineteen

Jared and Mel were at the back of the house trying to look through a window when they noticed movement to their right.

Instinctively, Jared snapped his head in that direction and openly gaped when Harper appeared on the lawn "What the ... ?"

Mel followed his gaze, dumbfounded. "What is she doing?"

"I don't know." Jared forgot he was supposed to be quiet and unobtrusive as he stood and straightened his shoulders. "Why was she in the woods?"

"Forget that. Who is she talking to?"

That's when Jared realized that Harper was indeed talking to herself, something he didn't notice until Mel pointed it out. Her lips were moving and she seemed agitated as she favored her hip and occasionally looked to her right as she walked.

"She found a ghost," Jared said after a beat. "It must be Jessica. Maybe she told her what happened and we can officially move."

The look Mel shot Jared was pitying. "Listen, I know you love your girlfriend and think she can do no wrong, but we can't secure a search warrant on the word of a ghost. You know that as well as I do."

"Yeah, but ... ." Jared trailed off, narrowing his eyes when Harper stormed right past them and continued toward the front of the house. "Did she not see us?"

Mel seemed equally puzzled. "I don't know. I ... thought she did. She didn't look at us, though. I guess it's possible she didn't. We were twenty feet away from her."

In tandem, they scurried toward the side of the house and peered around. Harper was still stomping toward the front door, her mouth moving a mile a minute as she talked to the ghost that apparently only she could see.

"I promise this will be over soon," she said. "You'll be on the other side in time for Christmas dinner."

"Jessica must not like being a ghost," Mel mused.

"Yeah, well, we need to figure out what Harper is doing," Jared said as he hurried to catch up with his obviously determined girlfriend. "She's going to draw attention and that won't bode well for us."

Mel grumbled something under his breath as he attempted to match Jared's pace. His partner couldn't decipher exactly what it was, but he didn't ask because he had other things on his mind. By the time the two men made it to the front porch, Harper was already up the stairs and standing in front of the door.

"Open up, you old witch!" Harper barked, kicking the door with her foot as hard as she could. "I know what you did. I know what you are."

Jared's mouth dropped open. "Harper," he hissed, his eyes flashing. "Get off that porch right now!"

Harper ignored him. "I can't believe this town treated you like a hero when you're pretty much the worst person ever," she groused, kicking the door again. "I mean ... what is the matter with you? Who does what you did? I just want to ... ." She broke off and mimed a violent act that Jared couldn't quite make out.

"Harper, you get off that porch right now," Mel ordered, his voice cracking. "I mean it. If she comes out and ... ." Whatever he said died on his lips because the door opened at that exact moment.

Shana, who wore a cotton night dress that zipped from throat to feet, didn't look happy to be interrupted. "Can I help you?"

"I certainly think you can," Harper said calmly, affixing a sweet smile to her face as she glared at the woman. "I want Zoe Mathers right now."

Curious despite himself, Jared watched the woman's face from the shadows. He expected Shana to feign confusion, or deny having Zoe outright. Instead, she merely glared at Harper with enough hatred to fuel a rocket ship.

"I believe it's a bit late for a visit, Harper," Shana said drily. "Perhaps you should stop by tomorrow."

"And perhaps you should bite me," Harper shot back. She was so disgusted there was no way she could back down now. "Where is Zoe?"

"I have no idea what you're talking about."

Harper tilted her head to the side, as if listening to someone. "Really?" she challenged finally. "I'm guessing that's not true. I'm guessing she's in the basement room nobody knows about, the one without windows. I think she's down there ... and I think she's crying for her mother."

The flash of fear that flitted across Shana's face caused Jared to take a step forward. He recognized savagery when he saw it, and there was no doubt in his mind that Shana was about to turn her fury on Harper. The question was: Did Harper realize it, too?

"I'm going to ask you to leave now." Shana's tone was icy. "If you don't, I'll have to call the police."

"I think that's a grand idea," Harper said, her smile more of a grimace as it washed over her features. "You call the police and get them out here. We're going to need them."

Jared wasn't surprised when Shana remained in the doorway instead of retreating into the house to make the call. The woman didn't want the police at her house. She was bluffing, and now that Harper had called her bluff, there was only one thing to do. All Jared had to wait for was Shana to make a move, then he had just cause for entering the home.

"If you don't shut your mouth, I'm going to shut it for you," Shana hissed.

"I'm not afraid of you." Harper was firm. "I know what you did. I know about Chloe."

Whatever Jared and Mel were expecting, it wasn't that. They exchanged a quick look, something unsaid passing between them, and then edged forward so they could hear the next part of the conversation.

Shana wrinkled her nose. "Everyone knows what happened to Chloe. It was a tragedy."

"Everyone knows what you told them," Harper countered. "They don't know that you were abusing Chloe, that you like absolute silence and reverence and are willing to mete out pain to get it. They don't know you hit her with a frying pan because she wanted to go to prom and then locked her in the quiet place in the woods behind the house."

Shana's face drained until she was so white she looked like a ghost herself. "W-what?"

"You heard me!" Harper was furious. "She had a head injury and you left her out there to die. She's still out there. You killed your own daughter and then played the victim. You make me want to throw up on your face."

As far as insults go, it wasn't her best offering, but Jared had to give her credit for holding it together despite everything that had obviously happened over the last twenty minutes. Shana, on the other hand, didn't look happy.

"I have no idea what you're talking about." She moved to shut the door in Harper's face, but Whisper Cove's favorite ghost hunter was having none of it.

"Stop!" Harper slammed her foot in the opening so Shana couldn't lock her out. "You're done here. This whole thing is done."

"You don't know what you're talking about," Shana screeched, doubling her efforts. "You're trying to stick your nose in my world and it doesn't belong. You're going to be sorry if you're not careful. In fact ... ." Shana stopped fighting and eased her pressure on the door, which meant Harper went tumbling inside.

That was enough for Jared. He broke into a run and headed straight for the porch, his weapon drawn. Mel was close on his heels.

"Why couldn't you just mind your own business?" Shana screeched as she tried to wrestle Harper to the ground. "Why did you have to stick your nose into something that doesn't concern you? I mean … what is wrong with you?"

Harper was livid. "You're a murdering jerk! The things you did to Chloe … you didn't deserve her."

"Chloe couldn't follow rules," Shana growled, grabbing a handful of Harper's hair and tugging viciously. "All she had to do was follow the rules. She was so stupid she kept forgetting. Well, that eventually came back to bite her, didn't it?"

Jared's mouth dropped open when he reached the top of the porch stairs and took in the scene. "What are you doing?"

"She's a murderer," Harper spat, slamming her hand into Shana's stomach and causing the woman's eyes to bug out of her head as she gasped for air. "She killed Chloe. I found her body in a shed in the woods. She has Zoe."

"Are you sure?" Mel asked, hopping into the fray and grabbing Shana's arms to keep her from lashing out at Harper. "Are you absolutely sure?"

Harper nodded without hesitation as she hopped to her feet. "I'm sure." She left Mel to cuff a belligerent Shana as she walked through the house, Jared close on her heels.

"Heart, I don't want to tell you your business, but I hope you're right about this," Jared said as they found the stairs that led to the basement. "If not, we're all going to be in a world of trouble."

"I'm right." Harper was so sure of that, she practically skipped down the stairs. "I know I'm right. In fact … ." She stilled at the bottom of the steps long enough to scan the basement. It was a hoarder's wet dream, items piled against each wall in every direction. There was only one additional door, though, and that's where Harper headed now.

"Zoe?" She called out, reaching for the door handle. It was locked. "Zoe, can you hear me?"

"You can't be sure she's in there," Jared said quietly, his heart going out to her. "I'm sorry. Maybe she's … ."

There was a response before he could finish. "I want to go home," a little voice announced from the other side of the door as tears ate the last word. "I want my mom," she wailed.

Jared's eyes widened. "Holy … ."

"I told you." Harper wasn't smug, just determined. "Open the door, Jared. Call her mother."

Jared simply nodded and leaned forward. "Zoe, I need you to take a step away from the door. I'm going to kick it in and I don't want you to get hurt. Do you understand me?"

"Who are you?"

"I'm the police."

"And you're going to take me home?"

"I am," Jared promised. "Just as soon as I get you out of there. Are you away from the door?"

"I'm in the corner."

"Here I come." Jared raised his foot and planted it on the door directly next to the locking mechanism. It sprung open to reveal a tiny girl in a pink jumper with tears flowing down her cheeks.

Zoe didn't wait for Harper and Jared to go to her. Instead, she strode straight through the opening and knuckled her eyes. "I want my mom."

Harper opened her arms and swept up the child without invitation. "Then let's give her the Christmas surprise to end all surprises, shall we?"

Zoe nodded, tearful. "I didn't miss Christmas, did I?"

Harper smiled. "Nope. You still have time, and something tells me you're going to have the best Christmas ever."

"I hope so." Zoe wrapped her arms around Harper, seemingly content to trust her, and didn't speak again until they were walking out of the house. Her gaze was dark when it landed on a furious Shana, who was cuffed and on her knees as Mel read her rights out loud. "She's mean."

"She's going to be punished for it, Zoe," Jared promised. "She's not going to get away with it."

"Good."

IT ONLY TOOK HARPER and Jared ten minutes to get to Ally's house. They had to wait for backup so Mel wouldn't be left alone. The uniformed officers who arrived were warned there was a shed in the woods that required a medical examiner and then informed they weren't to touch anything until the state police showed up with a crime team.

"I know my rights," Shana screeched. "You didn't have a search warrant."

"We didn't need one," Mel replied calmly. "Once Ms. Harlow entered your home and you engaged in a scuffle, we had every right to make sure no one got hurt. If you don't believe us, I'm sure your lawyer will explain it to you."

"Oh, this is just … ." Shana's glare was searing. "I hate all of you!"

"Somehow I think we can live with that," Jared said drily.

They had to take it slow during the drive to Ally's house. Zoe was a small child who was required by law to sit in a special child seat … something they didn't have access to. Jared opted to pretend he didn't know the rule while Harper sat in the backseat with Zoe on her lap.

"Do you think Mommy missed me?" Zoe asked as Harper smoothed her hair.

"I *know* she did," Harper replied. "I saw how much she missed you. I think you're going to be the best Christmas gift she's ever gotten."

"I just want to see her."

"We're almost there."

Jared helped Harper and Zoe out of the car before leading them to Ally's front porch. He checked the steps himself to see if they were icy, and he was just about to raise his hand to knock on the door when it opened. To his utter surprise, Ally wasn't the one standing on the other side of the threshold. It was Luke, and he looked as if he'd seen better days.

"Why are you here so late?" He looked at Jared, completely missing the presence of Harper and Zoe. "Please don't tell me she's gone."

It took Jared a moment to recover from his surprise. "What are you doing here?"

"I'm with Ally," he replied simply. "I'm doing what I should've done three years ago. I … is she gone? Is Zoe … dead?"

Before Jared could answer, Zoe gave voice to a question of her own. "Who is that?"

Luke snapped his head in her direction, his eyes going wide as saucers. "Oh, my ... Zoe."

"Who is that?" Zoe repeated, looking to Harper for an answer. "I don't know him. Where is my mom?"

Luke's mouth worked but no sound came out. Thankfully, Ally picked that moment to join the fray on the front porch. Her eyes immediately went to Zoe, as if drawn there by a power greater than herself. The sound she made when she saw her child was something Harper was likely to never forget.

"Zoe!" Ally barreled past Jared and Luke and aimed straight for the little girl. "My baby!" She collected her from Harper, sobs erupting as she wrapped the child in an embrace so tight Harper worried that Zoe would suffocate. "Where did you find her? Where have you been, baby?"

"A mean lady had me," Zoe replied, a look of exasperation on her face as she struggled to squirm away from her mother. "The mean lady is with the police now."

"What mean lady?" Luke asked, flashing an uncertain smile for Zoe's benefit as the girl continued to stare at him over her mother's shoulder.

"Shana Hamilton," Jared replied. "It's a long story, but we don't believe Zoe has been hurt ... other than being locked in a basement room."

"With spiders," Zoe said on a shudder.

"Shana is in custody right now," Jared added. "She'll be charged with kidnapping, false imprisonment, and probably murder a few times over. It's going to take some time to get the full story, but we wanted to get Zoe to you before interrogating her."

"I don't know how to thank you." Tears coursed down Ally's face as she rocked back and forth. "You found my baby."

Jared shook his head slowly and pointed at Harper. "She found Zoe. She found Chloe Hamilton, too."

"What?" Luke's mouth dropped open. "She found Chloe, too? How?"

"Chloe is dead," Jared replied. "Shana killed her."

"Oh, my ... ." Ally tightened her grip on Zoe. "Thank you so much for finding her." The look she graced Harper with was enough to cause the blond ghost hunter to choke up. "You'll never know the gift you've given me. I'll never be able to thank you properly for this."

"You don't have to thank me." Harper was sincere as she swallowed the lump in her throat. "I did what was necessary."

Ally was having none of it. "You went above and beyond."

"Not really. I just wanted Zoe home with you for Christmas."

"Well, you definitely did that," Luke said, smiling at his daughter as Ally straightened. "Do you want to come in for something to drink?"

"I don't think we should," Jared replied. "We need to get back to the scene."

"Of course." Ally bobbed her head. "Still ... thank you both."

"Who are you?" Zoe asked Luke, her eyes roaming his face. "I've seen you before. You saw me with the pumpkins."

Luke nodded. "I did. I was watching you."

"He's your father," Ally said simply. "He came to be with me while we were looking for you."

"Really?" Zoe's eyes went wide with wonder. "Are you leaving again?"

Luke shook his head, firm. "No. Not again. I'm sorry I took so long to get back to you, though. I'm going to make it up to you." He was tentative as he opened his arms to her. Zoe, on the other hand, didn't seem worried about the new man in her life.

"Okay." She leaned over and let him take her in his arms. She put up with an extended hug, and then let loose a huge sigh as she focused on Harper. "I'm really hungry."

"Now would probably be the time to ask for pizza," Harper suggested, grinning at the flash of delight in the girl's eyes. "Something tells me you're going to get whatever you want tonight."

Zoe flashed a thumbs-up. "Awesome. Who wants McDonald's?"

"Come on, hero," Jared whispered in Harper's ear as he slung an arm around her shoulders and drew her away from the warm family scene. "I think it's time we made our escape."

Harper agreed. "We got her home in time for Christmas."

"We did, although you did the heavy lifting."

"We worked as a team."

"Yeah." He kissed her temple. "Now and forever. Come on. Let's see what Shana has to say for herself and then put this night behind us. It's almost Christmas. I can't wait to spend it together."

"That makes two of us."

Twenty

Jared was in a good mood when he let himself into the house the next afternoon. He had to report for work during the morning hours — mostly because he wanted to be part of the team that interrogated Shana — but he was officially clear until after Christmas now, and his mind had turned to other things.

The house was bustling with activity, Christmas carols booming from the speaker in the corner as Pam and Zander toiled over what looked to be a huge meal. He took a moment to watch the interaction, grinning when Zander barked at Pam regarding her attempts to baste the turkey.

"You're doing it wrong."

"I'll have you know that I've been basting turkeys since before you were born," Pam shot back.

"Apparently not the right way."

"Yeah, yeah, yeah." She waved off his complaints and rolled her eyes. "I think you should leave the turkey to me and worry about the sides."

"Or you could leave the turkey to me and I'll handle the sides, too."

"You're something of a control freak, aren't you?"

"You say that like it's a bad thing."

Jared chuckled as he shrugged out of his coat, his eyes going wide when the door behind him opened to allow Harper entrance. He had no idea she'd left the house. "Where have you been?" His tone was more accusatory than he intended, but he couldn't hide his surprise.

"I was handling a bit of work for Santa," Harper replied as she kicked off her boots.

"What work?"

"I took gifts over to Zoe."

"Oh." Jared was momentarily chastised. "I didn't know you were going to do that. I wish you would've waited for me."

"I wasn't sure when you would be back and I didn't want to add to your day. Besides, they're spending their first Christmas together as a family and so many people have stopped by with gifts that Zoe believes she's being rewarded for putting up with the mean lady."

Jared smirked, legitimately amused. "Well, I don't think that's the worst thing that's ever happened." He leaned forward and gave her a soft kiss. "Is Luke still there?"

Harper knew what he was really asking. "Yes. It looks like he slept on the couch. There was a pillow and blanket stacked there, although no one volunteered information no matter how hard I dug. I think they're taking it slow."

"Maybe Luke will get his act together."

"He was sitting on the floor in front of the tree when I got there," Harper supplied. "Zoe was on his lap reading a Christmas story. She seems comfortable with him, as if it's the most natural thing in the world for him to be there."

"And Luke?"

"He had apparently listened to the same story four times in a row. It's the only one Zoe knows by heart according to Ally. He told her she was the best reader ever when she finished. He might be better at the father thing than he ever gave himself credit for."

"I hope it works out." Jared carefully ordered Harper's hair as she tugged off her hat. "You've been outside." He pressed his hand to her cheek. "Your skin is a lot colder than it should be if you only ran a quick errand. Where else have you been?"

"I can see why you make the big bucks, Detective," she teased as she hung her coat on the rack. "You're right, though. I've been out to two other places."

"Where?"

"The woods by Shana's house and the park."

Understanding dawned on Jared. "Did you find both your ghosts?"

"I did, and they're gone now. I gave them a Christmas gift, too."

"That's because you've got a huge heart." He pulled her into his arms, swaying back and forth as he kissed her temple. "They'll be happier on the other side, right?"

"I've never been there, but that's my guess. Either way, it's better than clinging to this life when it can't give them anything. Chloe was happy to cross when I explained her mother would never be getting out of jail. She asked me to say goodbye for her."

"Are you going to?"

Harper shrugged. "Maybe. I don't think it really matters. Shana is obviously a sociopath and she doesn't feel remorse for what she did."

"She definitely doesn't," Jared agreed, resting his cheek against her forehead as the music changed to a slower number. "She's not sorry for what she did. She blames Ally for being a bad mother and letting Zoe out of her sight. She said she had things she wanted to teach Zoe, and she had big plans. Luckily for us, it was a spur-of-the-moment thing. She wasn't planning on instituting her curriculum until after Christmas.

"It probably helped that she had to make appearances around town, too," he continued. "She locked Zoe in the basement room when she was out of the house. That gave her less time to focus on Zoe and her inability to follow rules. She killed Jessica because she assumed we would focus on her. She wanted to make it look like a suicide, but Jessica put up a fight. She thought she could still get away with it once she planted Zoe's hat in Jessica's car. She was so focused on Jessica that she had no time to focus on Zoe."

Harper involuntarily shuddered when she got a mental image of what he wasn't saying. "How could we not know that a monster like that was in our midst?"

"I don't know. She was a good actress. She mimicked emotions."

"Yes, but we should've seen." Harper was adamant. "People recognized there was something wrong with her. We should've looked closer. Heck, I've never been comfortable around her. I just wish I would've found Chloe's ghost before last night."

"I very much doubt you were wandering around the woods behind Shana's house very often," Jared noted pragmatically. "You can't blame yourself."

"If we'd known ... ."

"If we'd known then there's every possibility Luke wouldn't have realized what a jerk he was being and tried to adjust his attitude," Jared interjected. "The way things went down might've saved a family."

"I don't believe that." Harper's smile was wan as she leaned back to study his face. "Jessica and I had a long talk before I helped her pass over. She says that Luke was considering asking Ally for a second chance before they broke up.

"You heard Zoe," she continued. "She saw Luke watching her at the pumpkin festival. He did it from afar, but he was already caving."

"Only three years too late."

"Better late than never, though, right?"

Jared sighed. "You're right." He rested his forehead against hers. "If we don't allow people the opportunity to change there's no reason for them to adjust their behavior. If Luke really wants to be a father, Ally is the one he needs to convince. It's not on us to act as judge and jury."

"Well said." Harper's lips curved as she leaned closer to him. "It's almost Christmas. We should focus on each other instead of the horror of the last few days. We've done everything we can do."

Not everything, Jared immediately thought. Not quite yet, but soon. "You're right." He graced her with a soft kiss. "When are your parents getting here for dinner?"

"I'm sure we'll hear the hell hounds barking around the neighborhood as a warning when they draw near."

"What do you want to do until then? Zander and my mother are taking over the kitchen, which means we have some time to ourselves."

"Let's watch *A Christmas Story*."

It was the one answer Jared wasn't expecting. "Seriously? That's my favorite Christmas movie."

"I know. You told me. I haven't seen it in years."

"And that's all you want to do?"

"For now."

"Then … let's do it." Jared dragged her toward the large recliner at the edge of the room. "It's kind of nice to let them do the cooking and relax, huh?"

Harper nodded as she climbed into the chair with him. "The perfect end to a perfect day."

Jared managed to swallow his chuckle. She hadn't seen perfect yet. Not even close.

EVEN THOUGH THEY WERE both stuffed after dinner, Jared convinced Harper to walk across the road to the new house. It was a quiet night, bitter cold, but it was so loud at the other house because of the arguing — and Zander's insistence on being Zander — that they needed a bit of alone time.

Harper was lost in thought when she entered, her mind on Zoe and what she was probably doing to enjoy the evening, and she pulled up short when she saw all the lit candles placed around the room. "What the … ?"

Jared smiled. He'd snuck over thirty minutes earlier when Shawn and Zander distracted Harper with a game of Christmas trivia and arranged the house so he could give her his surprise. "Take off your coat."

"Why?" Harper whipped her head in his direction. "What's going on?"

"Take off your coat," Jared repeated, this time putting a bit of effort behind the words.

Harper did as she was told, stripping out of the coat and boots before moving to the blanket stretched out on the floor in the middle of the candles. "Are we having a picnic?"

"Something like that," Jared replied, rubbing his sweaty palms over his jeans as he followed her. He'd been calm when he disappeared to handle the candles and set-up. He thought he was ready. Now that the moment was here, he was unbelievably nervous.

"Do you like it?"

Harper nodded dumbly. "It's beautiful. Zander is going to melt down if we try to spend the night over here, though. You know that, right?"

"Zander will survive."

"Yeah, but ... ." When Harper turned, she was confused. The spot where Jared had been standing only seconds before was empty. He was no longer on his feet, in fact. Instead, he was on one knee with a velvet box in his hands. He was also unbelievably pale. "What's going on?"

"What does it look like?"

"I ... ." Harper's heart seemingly skipped ten beats in a row. "Are you proposing?"

"If you let me get the question out."

"But ... yes." Harper dropped to her knees alongside him. "Yes. I'll marry you."

Jared scowled. "You have to let me propose before saying yes."

"Oh." Harper was appropriately abashed. "I'm sorry about that. I didn't mean to steal your thunder."

Jared waited a moment and then inclined his head. "You have to stand up. I'm the one who is supposed to be on one knee."

"Oh." Harper was flustered, her face red as she scrambled to a standing position. "Better?"

Even though it was a serious situation, Jared wanted to laugh. The proposal was so them. "Close enough."

"Okay. Get on with it. Although ... this is why Zander wouldn't tell me what you got me for Christmas. I wondered why he was being so tight-lipped when he's never met a secret he didn't want to blab. I'm going to kill him."

"Hey!" Jared snapped his fingers to get her attention. "Are you going to let me do this?"

Harper nodded, solemn.

"Good." He sucked in a breath. "I love you," he started, his mind suddenly going blank. He couldn't remember the words he'd been practicing over the course of the past two weeks. "Um ... I really love you."

"I love you, too," Harper offered helpfully.

"Yeah, but ... I forgot what I was going to say." Panic licked at Jared's heart. "How could I forget? You totally threw me off."

Harper giggled as she dropped to her knees a second time. "It doesn't matter. I know what you feel because I feel it, too." She pressed her hand to the spot above his heart. "I love you more than anything. I want to be with you forever."

"If you propose to me, we're going to fight," Jared warned. "That's still my job."

"Then ask me."

"Fine." He opened the box and grinned at the way her eyes widened. "Harper Harlow, will you make me the happiest man in the world and be my wife?"

Harper nodded, momentarily stunned by the size of the diamond.

"You have to say the word out loud!" a muffled voice yelled through the window on the other side of the room.

Jared jerked his head in that direction and rolled his eyes when he saw Zander, Shawn, his mother, and Harper's parents standing with their noses pressed against the window.

"Yes," Harper said finally, her voice cracking. "Yes. You're all I want."

Jared smiled as she threw her arms around him, closing his eyes as her warmth washed over him. "You're all that I want, too."

"It's about time," Zander yelled through the window. "I was starting to think it was never going to happen."

"Go away," Jared bellowed. "This is our moment ... and you're ruining it."

"Oh, puh-leez. I'm just as much a part of this moment as the two of you. You'd better clear some room on that blanket because I'm coming in."

Jared thought about fighting him, but he couldn't. The moment was perfect for them — all of them — so that's all that mattered.

"This isn't what I had planned," he lamented.

"But it's what works." Harper's eyes filled with tears as she slipped on the ring. "We're going to be really happy."

His heart, he was ashamed to admit, turned to total mush. "You have no idea. This is the start of a new adventure."

"I'm really looking forward to it."

"Me, too."

Made in United States
North Haven, CT
18 January 2024